When she rose in the morning the house at first seemed to be the same. The furniture was where it had always been. Nevertheless, she felt uneasy. It wasn't the unreal uneasiness of someone waking up in an empty house and having to summon all her objects about her in order to assure herself of her own existence. Nor was it the uneasiness of old age. Yet it was a fine summer's day. The sun shone through the curtains of her window. On the floor it turned to minute particles like water dancing . . .

She recognised with a sourness in her mouth the source of her uneasiness, that her house had become insecure. Though her furniture was there it might disappear at any moment. If only her son could be at home with her . . . What had the girl said? Something about the 'burning of houses'. She had heard of this before but it hadn't seemed possible to her. She never believed it would happen to her. Things like that happened to other people. Anyway, they just couldn't put people out of their houses, and then burn the houses down. No one had ever heard of that before. Not in the country . . .

Consider the Lilies (1968) was Iain Crichton Smith's first and still, perhaps, his best-known novel. Born on the Isle of Lewis in 1928, Smith was educated there and at the University of Aberdeen. As a sensitive and complex poet in both English and his native Gaelic, he published many collections of verse, from *The Long River* in 1955 to *A Life* in 1986. The latter volume looks back over his years in Lewis and Aberdeen, to remember a spell of National Service in the fifties, leading to his work as an English teacher in Clydebank, and from 1955 at the High School in Oban until his retirement in 1977. He was the recipient of a number of literary prizes, Scottish Arts Council Awards and fellowships, as well as the Queen's Jubilee Medal and, in 1980, an OBE. He died in 1998.

As well as a number of plays and short stories in Gaelic, Iain Crichton Smith produced nine collections of stories in English.

By Iain Crichton Smith

NOVELS

Consider the Lilies
The Last Summer
My Last Duchess
Goodbye, Mr Dixon
On the Island
An End to Autumn
A Field Full of Folk
The Search
The Tenement
In the Middle of the Wood
The Dream
An Honourable Death

SHORT STORIES

Survival Without Error
The Black and the Red
The Village
The Hermit and Other Stories
Murdo and Other Stories
Selected Short Stories
Listen to the Voice
Thoughts of Murdo

CONSIDER THE LILIES

Iain Crichton Smith

Introduced by Isobel Murray

WEIDENFELD *&* **NICOLSON**

For Stewart Conn and Giles Gordon

First published in Great Britain in 1968
by Victor Gollancz Ltd
This edition reissued by Weidenfeld & Nicolson in 2018
an imprint of The Orion Publishing Group Ltd
Carmelite House, 50 Victoria Embankment
London EC4Y 0DZ

An Hachette UK company

1 3 5 7 9 10 8 6 4 2

A CIP catalogue record for this book is available from the
British Library.

ISBN 978 1 4746 1182 4

Printed in Great Britain by Clays Ltd, Elcograf S.p.A.

www.orionbooks.co.uk

Introduction

In this century many Scots have started to discover their history, and the Highland Clearances have become a dominant theme and a potent myth in Scottish fiction. Iain Crichton Smith's brief but invaluable Preface to *Consider the Lilies* outlines the historical phenomenon and points to non-fictional accounts by John Prebble and Ian Grimble, but he denies that this is 'an historical novel', and rightly accentuates the most important aspect of the book, that it 'is a fictional study of one person, an old woman who is being evicted'.

But the jacket of the first edition boldly stated: 'This is a novel about the Highland Clearances', and it displayed appreciative comments from Prebble, Grimble, and Neil Gunn among others—an astute piece of publicity. Thus early readers of the book were somewhat pre-conditioned, and the novel has been seen as a historical novel of the Clearances ever since. This seems to me still a slightly misleading description. And it has helped to focus attention on questions of historical accuracy. Francis Russell Hart first set out the problem of anachronisms:

> The woman is old; her husband is long dead in the Peninsular campaign; yet the Strathnaver action of Sellar took place in 1814 and his trial was the year of Waterloo, when the historic Macleod was still an un-married youth.

Will such liberties taken with history spoil the reading experience for those who are aware of them? Hart continues:

> If none of this matters, then Smith might have avoided the distractions of anachronism by not having historic antagonists argue the issues of the Clearances in the old woman's little croft house and in her bewildered presence.

The answer is to recognize that Crichton Smith is a poet who draws on the past as a source of images and symbols, rather than the sort of novelist who depends on the disposition of facts and details to build a convincing picture of another time.

Other novelists have consciously set out to treat the Clearances: Neil Gunn's *Butcher's Broom* (1934) is concerned to show how the community and culture of Highlanders were destroyed or diminished by the evictions, and Fionn Mac Colla's *And the Cock Crew* (1945) passionately criticizes the Calvinist ideology and attitudes that in his opinion left the people so vulnerable. The theme of eviction and loss, treated sadly or angrily, informs books as different as George Mackay Brown's *Greenvoe* (1972) and Robin Jenkins's *Fergus Lamont* (1979). But I would argue that Crichton Smith in this novel most centrally treats a theme basic to his other work: the dangers of accepting any 'ideology', any system of beliefs. In this respect *Consider the Lilies* is closest to *And the Cock Crew*, for the ideology inevitably under attack here is certainly Scottish Calvinism. Crichton Smith has many times written about the effects that the rigidities of Scottish Calvinism have on the Scottish psyche, and his attacks are passionate and deeply felt, for his own childhood on the island of Lewis was spent very much under the shadow of the Free Church there: 'I hate anyone trying to control my mind,' he says.

But just as the Highland Clearances can be seen as one example of man's inhumanity to man, so Scottish Calvinism for Crichton Smith is only one example of all the ideologies which people can and do use to shelter behind. He distrusts the political beliefs of Hugh MacDiarmid as much as the religious ones of T.S. Eliot or the more individual belief-system of Yeats, and he sees ideology as a carapace, wanting to strip it away, to make man as nearly as possible a spontaneous human being. Of Mrs Scott he says 'she was to be broken out of her ideology to see how she could cope as a human being', and that is the central action of the book. The Clearances are chiefly important to Mrs Scott because in her extremity she perceives the falseness and hypocrisy of the minister and the way he and his church have presented

God to her. Towards the end she reflects, 'You couldn't judge God by his servants. As well as this, you could find God in those who weren't his servants.'

All this is communicated simply and subtly in the novel, in the rendering of Mrs Scott's simple human consciousness. As the author says himself, 'a lot of the things that I do are really almost like internal soliloquies', and Mrs Scott's inner life is a prime example, unusual only because in other books his characters are generally more educated and intellectual than this old woman. But when he says 'the human is the centre of everything I do', and 'what I think I can do best—analysing people's minds', he is pointing in my opinion to the central success of this book.

The mind of an old woman is a subject that Crichton Smith has returned to again and again in his poetry. He was the sickly one of three brothers brought up by a very narrow and rigid widow, and his physical weakness made him the main focus of her attention. He developed a picture of the sexes where men are often 'extended adolescents', rather like the husband in this novel, and women are stronger. 'I do deeply think women are stronger, more enduring than men.' Crichton Smith looked after his mother until she died. Images of joyless and harsh old women recur in a number of his poems, and yet he treats the subject with a dispassionate understanding which is extraordinary. On the other hand he has also questioned the motives of those who care for aged parents, and in 'Statement by a Responsible Spinster' and 'She Teaches Lear', for example, he cast doubt on traditional views of the virtues of of self sacrifice.

Mrs Scott's story is conveyed through her consciousness, but also through an almost poetic use of images. Early on we learn of her mother's abiding fear of hell, and of the harshness bred in the daughter by years of joyless, stoic caring for her mother. She remembers her mother long ago being gay and happy and loving music, but the enjoyment of life is replaced by the fear of hellfire. During these years, of course, the daughter is being programmed in the same direction. Both women's lives are tellingly encapsulated in the scene in Chapter Two where Mrs Scott remembers her reaction to Alasdair's proposal of marriage. She briefly 'danced about the room', but at the same time she 'knew she would never be so happy again'. Then she set about cleaning the house particularly thoroughly. Investigating an old chest containing mementoes of her parents, she found reports of her father's good conduct and, most memorably and significantly, 'she even found her mother's bridal dress crushed under the heavy Bible which was in double columns and had no pictures in it'.

Her marriage is fore-doomed. Her husband, happy and spontaneous, lives for the moment, while she, the religious one, lives in the past and the consciousness of sin, and is preoccupied with the future at the expense of the present. Double meaning is pervasive: when the one-armed elder tries to explain he is no longer capable of spontaneous heroism and has a wife and family to consider, he says ambiguously, 'The future has made me afraid.' He recognizes that the old woman is 'totally inflexible' and 'impossibly intolerant', and can do nothing for her.

Stark contrast is crucial in that confrontation and the others, but the book forces us to explore Mrs Scott's consciousness more sympathetically by starting with a contrast where we inevitably side with her. When Patrick Sellar pays his cursory visit giving notice of eviction in the first chapter, he is quite young, vigorous and powerful, speaking fast in English and riding a white horse, while she is old and frail, speaking slowly in Gaelic, slow in comprehension, submissive, and dressed in black. This means that we start with a consciousness of her loneliness, frailty and vulnerability, and only gradually become conscious of the harshness and rigidity with which she faces others, in a life built on a concept of God Himself as a harsh absentee landlord, undoubtedly bent on eviction.

So, I would argue that the novel is centrally preoccupied with religion. It registers Mrs Scott's being suddenly stripped of her outer shell, in the scene with the minister and her perception of his falseness. On the way to the manse her discovery of a dead sheep with a scavenging crow is intensely vivid and memorable. The ironic implications of the image are many: Christ called mankind his sheep and himself the Good Shepherd, and the minister should be Christ's representative

The old woman is asking him to prevent his human flock being driven out to be replaced by an animal flock. The greedily patient crow reflects badly on the minister, and reminds us of Loch and Sellar's treatment of the people generally. Mrs Scott's dramatic collapse after the minister 'thrust' her from his door, and her awakening, almost like a rebirth, in the Macleods' home, mean that she can now attempt, old as she is, to see life steadily and see it whole.

The character of Donald Macleod also illustrates religious themes. It is no accident that Crichton Smith tells us in his Preface: 'I have made him an atheist through there is no evidence that he was.' He is a means of introducing a commentary on the Clearances which is more general and incisive than any Mrs Scott would be capable of, and his opposition is not only to the evictors, but to the rigidities bred into the people. He hates Patrick Sellar certainly, but he also hates 'those interior Patrick Sellars with the faces of old Highlanders who evicted emotions and burnt down love'.

But of course it is not Christianity that Crichton Smith is opposing here; it is what he calls 'the Calvinist ideology'. Christianity has always preached both the law and the grace, in different balance in different times and churches; this novel opposes law, in so far as that means external compulsion, rigidity and limitation, but it celebrates grace, spontaneity, generosity. It is Donald Macleod who is the Good Samaritan here: atheist though he is, he loves his neighbour: 'we have to look after each other.' He lives by his own felt values, very near to the positive teachings of Jesus.

The whole book is of course permeated with religious ideas and images. The New Testament treatment of shepherds and sheep, reflecting the relationship of Christ and his church, makes the very essence of the Clearances ironic. The book of Revelation has a vision of Christ as the Lamb. And if Donald Macleod is the Good Samaritan, Patrick Sellar is repeatedly described as a man on a white horse. This is a complex and ambiguous echo of Revelation 19, 11–15, where the Word of God descends from heaven on a white horse to smite and punish, with all the fierceness and the wrath of God. The ambiguity of this image is deliberate, for Sellar was sometimes seen as the vehicle of God's wrath against sinful men, as the minister suggests to Mrs Scott. But no reader of *Consider the Lilies* will be surprised to learn that Crichton Smith's first treatment of this subject, in a Gaelic play, was an account of the trial of Patrick Sellar – in hell.

Isobel Murray

Quotations from Iain Crichton Smith not otherwise identified in the introduction are from an unpublished taped interview with Isobel Murray and Bob Tait, one of a series of conversations with Scottish authors sponsored by Aberdeen University Development Trust.

ONE

Her name was Mrs Scott and she was an old woman of about seventy. She was sitting on an old chair in front of her cottage when she saw the rider. The rider was Patrick Sellar, factor to the Duke of Sutherland, and he wasn't riding his horse very well, though he felt that in his position he ought to have a horse. He was an ex-lawyer, and horses aren't used to that kind of law. Also, it was a white horse which was one of the reasons why the old woman paid such particular attention to it.

She was just an old woman sitting in the sun watching a few hens scrabble in the dust, and she wasn't really thinking of anything. Dreaming perhaps: for as far as an old woman is concerned there is little difference between reality and dream. She might have been dreaming of her youth or of her son in Canada or of her husband who had been a soldier. Or she might have been watching the horse neither dreaming nor thinking, though half-noticing how it sheered its head away from its rider, its nostrils flaring. She was wearing black, and was very frail-looking.

She didn't know much about horses and she didn't know anything about Patrick Sellar. Nor, for that matter, did he know much about her. As far as he was concerned, she was a disposable object. As far as she was concerned, he was a stranger and to be treated with hospitality even though she was old.

At first she couldn't see him very well, for her sight was beginning to fail a little. All she could tell was that there was a white horse with a man riding it. As he came closer she saw that he was wearing a sort of blue uniform with gold buttons and that he was short and fat. He took a long time dismounting, for his horse didn't seem to be making it easy for him.

She could tell that he liked to feel dignified, even though he had small burning eyes.

She saw, when he was off his horse, that he carried a whip. Perhaps he had been using it on the animal. The horse, however, relieved of its burden, was very quiet and began calmly to chew grass though now and then it would toss its head in the air.

He came over to where she was sitting.

Because she had been taught to be courteous and obedient to her superiors she stood up. It wasn't easy, but she succeeded. She was surprised that he didn't tell her to sit down for some of his superiors did this. Some of them even meant it, and had a kind of careless politeness, which this man didn't have.

'Good day to the gentleman,' she said.

She expected him to say 'good day' in return but he only grunted.

'Will the gentleman go in?' she asked.

'All I have to say to you can be said here,' said the man.

But of course that wouldn't do. It wouldn't be polite to keep a stranger outside the house.

She went inside and waited for him to follow her, which he did. At first she felt a little dazed going inside, for the room was dark and slightly chilly after the warmth outside. She sat down on one of the two chairs. She noticed that the stranger didn't want to sit but she signed to him to do so and he sat on the bench, which was close to the door. He kept hitting his whip against the bench and even though this irritated her she didn't ask him to stop. He was, after all, a guest in her house. She waited in silence with her hands crossed for him to begin to speak, staring into the empty grate.

'I suppose you'll know why I am here,' he began.

And then she had a flash of revelation. Perhaps he had come about her pension. Her husband had been killed in the war in a place called Spain, and now that she came to think of it he had talked to her once of a man on a white horse.

'It is about the pension?' she asked.

'What pension?' he asked.

'The pension for my man,' she said, 'They said I would get a pension.'

She had also received a letter from the King which the elder had read to her. It was beautifully printed on very important-looking paper. Very thick paper, with very large print on it. It was very beautiful and it was nice and thoughtful of the King to have gone to such trouble, especially when he had so much to do. She had framed the paper and it was hanging in the other room – the only other room – at that moment. Her mind began to wander a little after he had told her it wasn't because of the pension that he was here. She had a picture of her husband dead on a foreign field. He was wearing the uniform the Duke of Sutherland had given his men, the volunteers for his regiment. Her husband had always been adventurous with a streak of the boy in him.

'I'll tell you what I came for,' said the fat little man thumping the bench with his whip.

She looked up: she had almost forgotten him. And suddenly she saw that his burning little eyes were those of an enemy. She couldn't think why this should be so. She was sure she had never seen him before in her life and she couldn't understand how she had offended him.

'Will the gentleman have a cup of tea?' she said, though that would mean setting and lighting a fire and she was very tired.

'No, I haven't time for tea.'

She didn't wonder why he didn't say 'Thank you' or 'Tapadh leibh' because sometimes they said it and sometimes not. It depended what mood they were in. Anyway, he wouldn't know any Gaelic.

She didn't particularly like the look of him. His head wasn't Highland. It was too heavy and the face was too fat and red, and the eyes in the head were small and burning.

'I came to tell you,' he was saying, 'that you'll have to leave the house.' When he said this she was looking at his lips. For such a heavy head and such red cheeks the lips were very thin. For that reason she didn't at first take in what he had said. As well as this she was distracted by the sound of the whip with the silver knob at the top of it hitting the bench.

After a while the words came back into her mind.

'I came to tell you that you'll have to leave the house.'

Of course the words didn't make any sense. What should she leave the house for?

It was ridiculous to say that she must leave the house. She had nowhere else to go and in any case she didn't want to go anywhere else. Perhaps he hadn't spoken the words after all, but when she looked at him he was staring at her and his lips were quivering with anger. She found this disturbing and surprising and felt that she had done something wrong.

'Is it the pension?' she asked tremulously. 'Is it because of the pension you said that?'

He looked at her in astonishment and said:

'No, of course it's not the pension. I don't know what you're talking about.'

So it wasn't the pension. Then perhaps she had offended him in some other way. She went back in her mind over the past few minutes, how he had come riding on his white horse, how he had dismounted, how she had offered him tea. But no, she couldn't think of anything she had done to offend him. In addition, she felt a dull pain beginning in her left knee – the sciatica again.

She raised her curdled face and listened to him.

'It's the Duke who sent me. The Duke. Do you know him?'

No, of course not, how could she know the Duke? She had seen him but she didn't know him. What a silly question. She had seen him in full regimentals with his recruiting clerk sitting at a table in the open air. On the table was a bag with a pile of coins. Her husband had got some of the coins when he joined the Duke's regiment. She had also seen the Duchess once, in the grounds of the Castle. But she didn't know them. Anyway, they were away from Sutherland most of the time, especially in the winter.

Once the Duchess had sent a man with some meal when the crops were bad. At first they thought they were going to get it free, but they had to pay for it some time afterwards when they'd forgotten about it. That was what made it worse. If they had told them at the time it wouldn't have been so bad. But they hadn't. So they decided that in future they wouldn't take any meal if it was offered. It wasn't easy

to pay it back. Perhaps the Duke and the Duchess hadn't
known about it. Perhaps the man had put the money in his
own pocket. Still, there was little they could do about it.
They could only complain to the man himself and he wasn't
going to tell his employers. Then, again, the Duke and the
Duchess might have known about it and if they had
complained to the man he might have said that they hadn't
given him any money. Then they would have been worse off
than before. It was best not to say anything.

'I'm sorry,' she said, 'the gentleman was speaking.'

'Of course I'm speaking. I'm saying that the Duke sent me
to put you out.'

She stood up very slowly and pulled the curtain across the
window, because the sun was in her eyes. Equally slowly she
sat down again.

She felt that her slow movements irritated the man. But
then he didn't know what it was to be old. You had to be old
to know what it was to be old. The earth began to pull at your
feet as if it wanted to get you inside, and the sooner the better.

'I don't understand,' she said in the half-darkness.

If only he would speak a little more slowly. He spoke faster
than the people she was used to.

Her visitor drew a deep breath.

'It's very simple,' he said, 'the Duke wants you out of here
because . . .'

'Is he wanting the house for himself?' she asked.

Her visitor laughed but it wasn't a good laugh. It was a
mocking laugh, the kind of laugh rich and grand people
laughed, especially rich clever people, who didn't make
allowances for you when you were old, and didn't understand
your language at all.

She didn't think that she was superior to her visitor
because she could speak in two languages, though not so well
in English as in Gaelic, whereas he knew only one. After all,
rich people and rich people's servants didn't know Gaelic:
that was the way it was.

'Imagine it,' he was saying, 'the Duke wanting this house!'

Well, true enough, the Duke lived in a castle but her house
wasn't a bad one either. She had a dresser and two chairs and
a bench and she had cups and saucers ranged on the dresser

and she had a table and a lamp. What more did you need?
But certainly the Duke lived in a castle just the same.

'No,' said her visitor, his laugh having stopped very
quickly. 'He's going to pull the house down.'

He said this as if it were the most ordinary thing in the
world. Pulling her house down, when after all it was her
house. She had never lived in any other house in all her
seventy years. On the death of her parents – she hadn't
married till they were both dead – her husband had come to
live in this house. She had been born in the house, had spent
her girlhood there, and had spent all the years of her marriage – such as they were – in it.

She couldn't exactly put it into words but she knew that if
she left the house she would die. Naturally, she hadn't long
to live anyway, perhaps five years, perhaps ten. But if she left
the house she would die. And anyway, there was no other
place for her to go. How could she sleep in any other bed
than the one she had? And who would carry the grandfather
clock away for her? No, it was out of the question. She
couldn't leave the house alive. But at the same time she
didn't have the words to explain all this to the visitor in the
way she would have liked. She might have said 'I'm too old'
or 'I'm seventy years old' but for some reason she didn't
want to appeal to his pity. She had her pride to keep. Her
husband had made one of the chairs himself with his own
hands. For a weakening moment she thought of the gaiety of
her early married days, after the long illness of her mother.
But she put the thought out of her mind as soon as it came.

'My mother used to sit in that chair,' she said.

At the end her mother had been very difficult. She
believed that she was going to hell, though no one knew what
had put that idea into her head. She would get up in the night
screaming that she was on fire. One night they had found her
in her nightgown by the banks of a loch. Was she going to
throw herself in, her face twisted in the light of the moon,
turned at bay like an animal without teeth but with very very
bright eyes? But of course her visitor wouldn't know about
this, nor the helpless overwhelming pity she had felt for her
mother. Nor did he know about those long patient years
which had put a hardness in her, a hardness which her

husband had often commented upon. Sometimes she had to fight against her own inflexible will when dealing with her son.

'How do you get on here anyway?' said her visitor. 'You seem to be on your own.'

'No,' she answered with panic, 'there's the neighbours; there's James the Elder, and there's Big Betty, and there's Annie. She gets the water for me.'

As well as that she went to church every Sunday. She liked going to church. In fact she wouldn't know what she would do if there was no church. She liked the minister because he talked well and told the truth. To speak well and sincerely was a great gift, and furthermore he was dignified and was said to be very learned. She also liked the silence of the church when she could sit there as in a cool well and feel all her troubles and sorrows and tensions unravelling themselves, leaving her quite clean and whole. She liked to be shaken by the hand by the minister when she was going out. It gave her the impression that she was someone, though she never looked the minister in the face during those brief conversations they had. He had very plump cheeks – this she could see when he was preaching – and a way of smacking his lips at the end of sentences. But the most striking thing about him was his dignity. She could rely on him, though she didn't have occasion to up until now.

'Of course it won't be exactly like this house,' her visitor was saying. 'In fact it will be better, cleaner and made of stone. You might even have a carpet on the floor.'

She got up again painfully and went over to the window. From there she could see the churchyard and some of the tombstones leaning towards each other. Her husband wasn't buried there but her father and mother were. She didn't even know whereabouts her husband was buried though it was in a place called Spain.

'What are you looking at?' said her visitor angrily. 'At your land? What good has it ever done you? It's all stone, isn't it? If you had any sense you wouldn't worry about leaving it. This new house will be in the north by the sea.'

But she wasn't looking at the land, she was looking at the churchyard.

'My father and mother are buried in the churchyard,' she said.

'Yes, you people are always talking about the dead.'

Well, why shouldn't they? The dead were always around them. Soon she herself would be dead. The dead just didn't go away for ever. They were near the house, present in the house. The bed she had was her father's and mother's marriage bed. The grandfather clock had been passed down through generations. Also, very few people would go near the churchyard at night. Did he think the dead went away for ever? Of course not. She remembered her own father dying, with his long white beard. He was a good age when he died, yet was as frightened as a child in the silent house. Her father and mother remained as presences in the house. So did her husband, even though he had died in another country. She remembered his small alert moustached face emerging dripping out of the basin of water.

'This is my father's house,' she said at last.

'I thought it belonged to you,' said her visitor quickly. 'We were told it belonged to you,' and then he stopped. 'But of course your father can't possibly be alive.'

Why 'of course'? Of course he was alive. People didn't die as easily as that. More than memories remained of them. There were the clothes and the objects they had used. The print of their hands was still on them. She hadn't been living in an empty house.

'Can the gentleman tell me why the Duke wants the house?'

'I've told you,' he almost screamed. 'He's going to pull it down. He needs the land for the sheep.'

She didn't understand half of what he was saying. She understood the last sentence, and so said:

'Sheep don't have souls. The gentleman knows that.'

'"The gentleman knows that",' he repeated. 'Why do you always talk in the third person?'

He stopped looking out of the window and began to speak another lot of words which she didn't take in much. She didn't need to, for he seemed to be speaking to himself.

'It's true I'm a servant of the Duke, but don't think I value him as much as you think. I may even value him less than you do. He had all the advantages. I haven't any. But I must be in London too. To have my own coach and my own horses and, by God, you're not going to stop me – nor a thousand like you.'

He turned violently away from the window and something about her bowed submissive posture seemed to irritate him even more for he lashed the whip against his leather leggings and said:

'Don't think you're going to stop me.'

He came towards her and spoke in a calmer voice.

'It's not as if you aren't getting a better house. As I have told you already, it will be cleaner and better-appointed than this. We'll even take your furniture up there for you. We're not brutes, you know. I can't understand why you don't accept such an offer at once.'

'The house belongs to my husband,' she said, 'and to my son.'

Something flickered at the back of his eyes.

'Your son? Where is your son? I didn't hear anything of a son.'

'In Canada. My son is in Canada.'

Married to a wife she'd never see. With children she'd never see. He turned away then, as confident as ever.

She considered for a long time knowing that something was wrong. Then she turned round and said:

'But the sheep aren't needing houses to live in. The sheep graze on the grass.'

She sat down. And he stood up, speaking very slowly as if through gritted teeth.

'No,' he said, 'sheep don't need houses. But they need land. And they need your land. And this house is in their way. Do you understand that?'

One would think that it was he himself who was demanding the land, yet he was only a servant of the Duke. Why therefore was he so angry? What did it have to do with him? She wanted to pass her hands wearily over her eyes, as he paced violently up and down, but she kept them crossed in her lap as he spoke.

'You've never been to London, have you? Of course not. But I have. It is a city full of lights, and big houses, and coaches. You can go to the theatre and to concerts and to gaming houses. You don't know about that. How could you? What comparison has this little village with London? What civilisation do you have here? What do you do but plant and sow and reap, year in, year out? What sort of life is that? Tell me.'

Her eyes shuttled back and forth, following him on his frantic pacing as if he were a caged animal.

'Do you think I want to live here? Why do you want to live here? Why does anyone? This is an animal life. You people never see anybody new from one year's end to another. You never see anything new either. And you think about hell all the time. Well, what are your lives but a living hell? You talk to me about sheep. What are you but sheep?'

What was he saying about a living hell? What did he mean?

'What would I be doing in another house?' she asked.

She tried to recall when she had last been away from this one, but could only remember the one instance when she had gone to see her sister at a place about five miles away. No, it was just like a potato. You tore it away by the roots and soon it would rot. It was natural for a potato to grow in the earth. If you took it out of the earth before its time it would die.

'Look,' he began. 'I didn't live here always. I come from a place a good distance away. Does that mean I'm not happy here? Of course not. Naturally I sometimes remember the place I came from, but I came to this place. My work brought me here. You're going to a better place too. Perhaps in a year or two I'll be moving to another place.'

But she couldn't think of any place she could go to. To go somewhere else would mean taking this place with her, and she couldn't do that. How could anyone do that? She remembered a dog her husband had got once. It had run back to where it came from. They had let it go. Why, even animals didn't like being moved about.

'My man wouldn't like the new place,' she said. 'He'd say: "I can't come in with my dirty boots." That's what he'd say.'

'I thought you said your man – your husband – was dead.'

'He's dead, but he wouldn't like it just the same.'

Why couldn't this man understand the simplest things?

You had to keep telling him things which he ought to know already, things which everybody knew. It was very tiring. She made an effort. 'And anyway, there's no church up there.'

He looked at her triumphantly: 'The church is being pulled down as well.'

She was looking at a square of sunlight on the floor. In the middle of it she noticed a patch of grey. Funny how she hadn't noticed that before. She tried to think what had caused it and was angry with herself because she couldn't think of it, in the same way as she was angry when she couldn't remember someone's name. She pecked at a memory just on the very edge of her mind as hard as she could. What an effort it was to remember anything these days. There was a time when she could tell you everyone's genealogy and what part of the country he or she came from and what his or her relations had died of, even sometimes in what month of the year he or she had been born. But she couldn't think what had caused that grey patch. She was irritated with the sunlight for revealing it so clearly.

But what had he just said? Something about the church being pulled down. That of course was untrue. He must be joking. Who had ever heard of a church being pulled down? At least she hadn't heard of this happening. And she was sure the minister wouldn't allow it. Or the elder.

'I'm sorry,' she said. 'The gentleman said they were going to pull the church down.'

'It's true enough,' said her visitor, tapping the whip against his legs. 'We'll pull it down stone by stone and then we'll take it up to where the new village is going to be. And your minister will go up there as well.'

What was he talking about? Stone by stone? What did he mean by it? Surely he must be making fun of her. But she wished he would go away just the same. Inside herself she was praying: 'Please God don't let him take the house away from me. Don't let him take the house away from me.'

Then she was angry with herself. God wouldn't let him do it. God wouldn't let him take the church away either. God was stronger than anyone, stronger even than the Duke. God who had saved her mother at the end when she was going to kill herself after thinking she was going to hell.

'God won't let you,' she heard herself saying.

And he laughed. He just laughed and didn't say anything. Naturally she didn't expect God to strike him down there and then. After all, the rich and the servants of the rich often laughed at God and nothing happened to them at the moment they did it. But they paid for it in the end. God would not be mocked. On their death-beds they paid for it. If not before. And if not then or before, afterwards.

'I don't want your house,' she said. 'And tell the Duke, he can keep the pension if that's what's worrying him.

'This house is full of my people's blood.'

'You'll have to leave just the same,' he said, rising.

'God won't let you put me out,' she said.

Now she remembered. That grey spot must have been caused by the milk she had spilt hot from the pot. That was it. The hot milk from the pot. She must get a scrubber and scrub it clean.

'You haven't got much longer,' said her visitor at the door. 'And remember what I told you. You'll get a new house. Don't worry about that. But you'll have to get out. You haven't got more than a week.'

She wanted to ask her visitor if he was married, but didn't dare. He didn't act as if he were married, or had suffered the pains of life. If he had had the Gaelic she might have been able to speak to him properly. But then he was clever and she was not. And even if he had had the Gaelic he might not have been able to understand, for he seemed to be quite young. And she herself hadn't understood her parents very well, though she did understand them a little at the end.

TWO

After the man on the white horse had departed she made a fire, boiled water, and scrubbed the floor. She did this though she was very tired but the scrubbing made her a little less tired. She didn't get the greyness out but she felt more contented – at least she'd tried.

When she had finished the scrubbing and poured the dirty water into the grass in front of the house, she made herself some tea and ate some of the scones she had made on her griddle. Then she sat down on the chair in front of the fire, her old bones aching. It was beginning to grow dusk and the room was steadily darkening like a well filling slowly with water. Her knee ached as before and so did her back now. Her hands were chapped with the hot water.

She began to think vaguely of the events of the day, but was too tired to think what she could do about them, though she knew she would have to do something very soon. She was not so old that she hadn't heard about the sheep, though at the same time she had never believed that because of them anyone would come to put her out. After all, she was an old woman who lived alone and she wasn't troubling anyone.

She spent her days as follows. She woke in the morning, made her breakfast, took the cow out to graze, cleaned the house, sat about in the good weather in the sun, made her dinner, sometimes had a neighbour in, and went to bed early. On Sundays she went to church and on Wednesdays to prayer-meetings.

She didn't have the power to hurt anyone any more. Sometimes she got a letter from her son in Canada. Reading between the lines she knew that life hadn't been easy for him. She had heard of the bad rocky land and the deceitful agents who had taken them across the sea. But he was young and would survive. Life was always difficult and one didn't expect luxury.

As she lay half-dozing in the chair pictures swam in front of her closed eyes. Most were pictures from her youth for as one grows older one remembers most clearly the distant days, childhood and girlhood and wifehood. This particular evening there seemed to be more pictures than before. Pictures of her father, her mother, her husband. Not all were pleasant: many were not. But for some reason they emerged with a more prolific clarity. She remembered, for instance, the nights they used to dance to the music of the melodeon. This was before her mother had grown old and crabbed and half mad with fear. After all, her mother hadn't always been like that. She used to wear sweet-smelling clothes and aprons covered with flour. She used to stamp blankets in the white water – gaily as a girl. And there were the days they used to pick potatoes, the treasures of the earth, the white ones and the sliced rainbow-coloured ones.

Voices came and went behind her head in front of the flickering fire. And music, the music of the melodeon. The melodeon was played for the dances at night at the end of the road, when the red autumn moon was ripe in the sky, the moon of 'the ripening of the barley'. She could hear the sudden whoops of the dancers as they danced the eightsome reel, one of the commonest dances. At that time she would have been fifteen or sixteen. Surely there was no harm in the dancing? What other pleasures did they have, except the telling of stories in each other's houses, the ceilidhs? Her mother had put a stop to all that – the dances, the ceilidhs. No one could tell how she had become possessed by the fear of hell in her latter days. During her early years she had been on the whole bright and cheerful. People often became melancholy in their old age.

Towards the end of her life her mother read the Bible all the time, looking for signs and sayings. When her eyes had become too bad for reading she herself had to read chapter after chapter to her. This was the only way she could get her to sleep. For this reason she knew long snatches of the Bible by heart, all about Joseph and his brothers, and Ruth and Naomi, and Saul and David.

Her other sister had cleared off to get married, had left her to bear the burden alone. Not that she ever had any intention of laying down the burden. In the Highlands one got used to bearing burdens. In the morning she would milk the cow, bake bread, and make crowdie. Later she would make the dinner. After that she would clean the house and sometimes her mother in her shawl would come and sit in the chair by the fire. Latterly this didn't happen, and she would sometimes shout instructions to her from the bedroom. In the evening she would sit and listen to her mother's stories, disjointed bits and pieces which were difficult to follow since the characters would jump generations with no warning, and anyway she herself only half-listened. How could one pay attention to all that, endlessly? Her mother liked to talk, simply for the sake of talking. Sometimes a neighbour might come in the evening – Big Betty, for instance, jovial and ribald, and deaf enough for her to speak loudly to everyone, as if it were they who couldn't hear her.

At night she herself would lie in bed, listening to the music of the accordion and waiting for her mother's death. Her father had died some years before. One day he had come in from the field. Blood had begun to pour from his nose, after he had bent to take his boots off. The blood had poured down his beard and right down his jersey in an absolute river. He had taken to his bed, badly frightened, and had never risen from it. On a cold winter's night of a cold moon he had died. By that time his nose had turned thin and blue and his voice had become very gentle.

That left her with her mother who had died when she herself was twenty-nine. On the night of the day of her mother's burial, she went to bed and slept for twenty-four hours. The day had whirled round her, still lying in her bed, illuminating her pale hair and thin face. When she awoke and got up the house was empty. For hours she sat there waiting to hear her mother's call from the other room. No one came. Yet her mother's presence was absolutely palpable in the house. At night she was frightened to go to bed lest in the empty house at midnight she would see her mother in her nightgown standing furiously by the bedside. But she real- ised she must stay in the house all night and not be frightened. After the first night she relaxed more, though never completely.

Emerging into the day was like entering a hurtful world where the light hurt her eyes. In those first days she ate little and sometimes did without food altogether. She walked like a convalescent over an earth heaving at her feet. However, she was fortunate that it was the time for cutting the peats. Alasdair came over to do the cutting for her. He was four years younger than she, with a small head and moustache, and quick movements. She couldn't of course pay him in money but would herself help at carrying the peats home for Alasdair's family. She couldn't do the cutting herself: that was a job for the men.

Alasdair was for ever singing. In the morning with the ascent of the lark his voice could be heard raised in song all over the village. There had always been an adventurous quality about him, and he was given to the practical jokes common to all small villages. Like, for instance, the time he had driven Big Murdo's cart away in the middle of the night at Halloween and no one could find it. Later it appeared as mysteriously as it had disappeared.

It was strange and joyful to have someone young in the house again. She made him a good breakfast before he went off cheerily to cut the peats in his boots and neat navy blue dungarees, his hair sleeked back, his face with the cultivated moustache very bright. He ate well but rather hurriedly, she thought, not with the heavy deliberation of her father.

She followed him with her eyes as he strode over the moor in the early summer morning, heavy with dew. For some reason she thought of the nests of larks which they used to find quite easily near the tracks made by the carts: and of the yellow beaks of the nestlings. She heard herself singing as she made dinner for him. She went to the door to see him coming and was surprised to find him home earlier than she had expected. He had wrapped a handkerchief round his head because it was so hot – the sweat had been falling into his eyes – and clowned a little. She poured out cold water for him in a basin and took pleasure in watching him splash it on his head before he sat down to his dinner. She had put on her good dress, the black one that showed her pale hair and pale face.

At dinner time there was a little constraint but she piled more and more potatoes on his plate. The house seemed full of sun which laid squares of light on the floor and made yellow tracks across his hair. They talked of Norah who was getting married. He himself had two unmarried sisters in a small house. As well as that, his father and mother were alive.

She heard him saying, eating as he did so, 'I suppose you've had a bad time,' and longed to tell him about it but didn't because of her pride. Anyway, he was eating. He had very generous impulses. Sometimes she caught him looking around the house and down to the fields. After his dinner he took out his pipe and began to smoke. Again she thought he was unlike her father, who smoked very slowly. Alasdair smoked in quick puffs.

'It's going to be a good year for the crops,' he said. It was indeed. After he had smoked a little he went off again, walking very quickly, wanting to be finished.

She had seen him often in church sitting up perfectly straight in his seat, always looking neat and perfectly aware of it. He laughed a lot when he got outside and made jokes.

In the evening she found herself thinking of him, for the house seemed even emptier than before, cold and silent. She ate very little, being on her own, and wondered what it would be like to be married. Not that this was the first time she had wondered this. But to be married was a happiness beyond her aspiration.

She looked in the mirror at her fair hair and pale face. She certainly wasn't ugly and the signs of suffering endured had made her face interesting and mature. No, she wasn't ugly but had he noticed that? Later he came with the 'crew' to take the peats home. On that day there was much laughter as they gathered round the cart pitching the peats up. He – who else? – stacked them quickly and neatly, his hair stirring a little in the breeze, his face darkened by the peat dust. Big Betty made a few remarks about them which were received with much friendly laughter. She couldn't remember any of the remarks now, but she remembered the happy atmosphere of the day. They sat by the peat-stack dashing the midges out of their eyes. Their long skirts trailed the ground

and their brows were wet and prickly with sweat. Little Iain
was allowed to walk beside the horse and looked very
important as he did so. They indulged their children, these
women, but could be severe on them too.

As they made the dinner at her house for the 'crew' she
was told by Big Betty: 'You two should get married.'

She blushed but didn't say anything.

'What's the use of you sitting in this empty house alone?'
said Betty. 'A house should have a man in it. A man to cut
the peats and the corn, and to thatch the house.'

True, it wasn't easy for a single woman. But what could
she do? She couldn't go up to him and say: 'Will you marry
me?' He was always the life and soul of the party, singing as
he caught the peats and composing spontaneous little
poems. He looked all fire and energy as he stood there, high
above everyone else, loving it in the sunshine.

After that they found themselves increasingly coming
from church together. She liked going to church and always
had done. Now that she was 'free' she liked going more than
ever. It was some time before she realised that one of the
reasons why she liked it so much was because she wanted to
get away from the empty house.

She knew, however, that Alasdair wasn't very interested
in religion or prayer. He just liked going because he could
put on his best suit and meet people. They would walk
home together in the quiet of the evening. In the distance
she could see the misty blue hills. She could hear the quiet
murmur of the waters. It was all like a picture. One night he
saw her home and standing by the door, his hat in his hand,
he asked her to marry him.

'I'm getting to twenty-five, now,' he said. 'It's time I
settled down.' His eyes glanced at her sparklingly and
restlessly. And he laughed gaily. She thought he laughed
rather much for such a weighty matter, but at the same time
she judged that he might be nervous. She had never been so
happy in her life.

When she got inside she danced about the room. She
picked up the picture of her father, gazed at it and laid it
down again. Her heart was brimming like a cup which could
hardly contain its happiness. Yet at the same time she knew

she would never be so happy again.

That night she cleaned the whole house from top to bottom. She found at the bottom of an old chest a picture of her father and mother, her mother seated, her father standing behind her. His hands were big and he had a beard. She looked placid, her hands folded in her lap. Her smile was uncertain and hovering. The picture was brown with age. She put it away, then found a book which told of her father's sailing days:

Conduct – Good.

Conduct – Very Good.

Conduct – Excellent.

The writing of this was blurred and the cover dog-eared. She found a ring belonging to her mother and a Bible, in the front of which were written various names:

Georgina Scott – born 1701

Mary Scott – born 1730

She even found her mother's bridal dress crushed under the heavy Bible, which was in double columns and had no pictures in it. She liked pictures in Bibles. It was a very big Bible. One could never dream of carrying it to church. It was too heavy for that.

She also found an old navy blue cap with braid along the edges. Funny how she had never examined the chest while her parents were alive. And there was a piece of carved wood which seemed to be a leg of something. At first she couldn't understand what it was, then realised it was one of the legs of a cradle. She left it lying on the top. After a while she closed the lid of the chest but cleaned the dust from it.

Then she made the bed all over again and changed the clothes. She cleaned the grandfather clock, and was interrupted once by a terrific boom which seemed to shake its old body to the very bones. She scrubbed the table and the chairs and the wood of the bed. She cleaned the bedroom window. All the while she hummed to herself. She even went into the barn and spoke to the cow, putting her arm around its neck while it gazed back at her with large liquid eyes. No, animals couldn't know such happiness.

All the night she tossed and turned and couldn't sleep. The house seemed to be full of vague moonlight presences.

She thought of getting up and going for a walk but thought of her mother and didn't. The night was calm and the moon shone warmly all by itself in the empty sky. In the early hours of the morning she was still awake, as if waiting for a message from her parents. But there was none, and near dawn she fell asleep, to wake when the sun awoke her. She felt like a bird, the heart throbbing in her breast so that she had to put her hand on it to steady it.

But she didn't go and tell anyone of her happiness, for her nature was secretive. So she hoarded it like a pail full of sparkling water in a dark corner.

They were married and after that life began.

And she began to find out about a totally new person, one who had not grown with her, one who came from outside, from a similar yet totally different world. He was not at all like her father. He was not deliberate and grave. He lived, unlike herself, from moment to moment, flashing like water in the sunlight or like tears. It was she who had to think what future they would have. He never seemed to think of it at all.

But she found out soon enough that the dark years had cast their shadow on her. In those long nights, when her mother fitfully slept, she had taken to brooding about the future. She had wondered what would happen to her if, for instance, her mother lived for another ten years. She had seen herself forever alone in an empty house. And she had been, though not consciously, preparing for those years. For instance, she spent little on herself and saved all the money she could. She had trained herself too to save her emotions. When her mother cried out of the dark, and in terrifying moments called on her own mother, she had trained herself to rise slowly and calmly from her bed. Sometimes she did not rise at all. For what could she do? In self-defence she let a part of herself die. How otherwise would she have survived?

But her husband had been playing football or going to dances when she was struggling with these nightmares. Even yet if he had a chance he would play with the 'boys'. The truth was she was much older than he in suffering and her insight into the human heart on the verge of madness. And in those days she was jealous of him – jealous of his spontaneity and his forgetfulness, of his seemingly motiveless swings from grave to gay and back again. She found him as uncomplicated and natural as a child.

She thought marriage demanded a greater sense of responsibility than this. She was, for instance, meticulous about the cleanliness of the house. She wouldn't say anything directly to him when he threw his boots under the table and flung his stained jersey on the table. But her silences were meant to be disapproving. He would stay in bed later than she liked, and go to it at night very late. She had made a practice of going to bed at ten o'clock at night or earlier, for what was there to stay up for? Nevertheless, what had begun as a reaction against emptiness remained as a habit which had taken her to its heart.

When the child came he was very fond of him, and very proud. He would lift young Iain to his shoulders and take him along in his woollen dress to show to their neighbour, Donald Gunn. He would boast, telling Donald how clever Iain was in comparison with young Murdo Gunn. This, of course, was only friendly rivalry. Nevertheless she disapproved of such excesses. And in those days she was convinced that she was in the right, he in the wrong.

He would coddle the child but she was much sterner. Inevitably, the child preferred him to her. This rankled with her for she considered it very unfair. She was thinking more of its long-term interests. That was why as he grew up she didn't want him to run into danger, why she limited his expeditions, why she read to him from the Bible – while her husband would play football with him.

The first time she knew that something was seriously wrong was when Alasdair came in drunk. She ignored him in cold fury but he did not wish to be ignored. He kicked the door shut and stood in the middle of the room shouting. She had never seen anyone drunk in the house before. It was a different Alasdair she was seeing, not the bright clown but an almost crazy red-eyed drooling half-maniac. That was the night he had taken her father's picture from the wall and thrown it across the room.

'Can't stand it any more,' he was shouting endlessly. 'Can't stand it.'

She put his plate of porridge before him, not speaking and not knowing what to do.

'You hate everybody. You hate to see anybody enjoying themselves.'

Silence.

'Even children. You hate to see children enjoying themselves.'

Silence.

'Not going to put up with it.' Then, in a grotesque imitation of her voice: 'Boots by the fire.'

In another imitation: 'You don't know you were born . . .'

Then he collapsed into silence, leaning back against the chair while he muttered to himself over and over:

'You hate everybody.'

After he had repeated that for a long time he fell asleep, snoring. She went to bed and left him there.

In the morning he was very repentant and kept looking at her as if wishing that he could be forgiven. She made no reference to the events of the previous night. Inside herself she was thinking: I wish I could tell him it's all forgotten. I wish I could show him I don't care. But that part of herself had been burnt out and she had lost the power of being spontaneous. But was it her fault? Could he not see what she had suffered all these years? But of course he couldn't, he hadn't experienced these sufferings. It was impossible for him to understand, though his wary glances sometimes suggested that there was something to understand. After all, he had had no responsibilities. It wasn't in him to sacrifice himself as she had done. He would have been unable and possibly unwilling to do it. As she saw him playing with the child she sometimes wondered whether his way was not the best after all. Shortly afterwards she would put that out of her mind as if it were a devilish thought.

One day he came in and said: 'I'm going to join the Army.'

And she knew within herself that this was what he would do, that this was what his whole life had been leading up to. He was too restless to stay in the one place all his life. Too adventurous, too irresponsible. Too much of a little boy. She imagined him in his proper place all dressed up behind the pipes and drums, letting the crowds admire him, living in the moment. It had taken him a little time to discover his place but now that he had he would wish to leave her.

Her first instinct was to keep him at home, for her will was stronger than his. She could calculate, and attack him at his weakest point. She could keep on and on. He wouldn't be able to do this to her. She had the child to bring up. It wouldn't be easy. And she foresaw clearly that as soon as he left home he would to all intents and purposes forget about her and it, no matter how gaily and affectionately he played with it now.

When it came into his head he would write 'a few lines'. Perhaps he would see someone who reminded him of her, some black-gowned foreign woman, and then he would say, 'I must write'. But as for keeping her continually in his mind she couldn't expect that of him. He would become completely involved in his soldiery, in the glitter and glamour of war. He would move into the future like a sparkling river, completely careless, not worrying where he was going, not even realising that he was falling from level to level, bemused by the sudden flashes and the wayward innocent sounds. All this she knew, yet let him go.

On the appointed day they went along with one or two others to the recruiting table. The Duke made a short speech. She listened but wasn't deceived by it. What were these countries to her? And that man on the white horse – what did she care about him?

But she saw that to Alasdair the words were like a trumpet call. He saw new countries ahead of him, new adventures. He was like a child wanting to do things which he wasn't sure were quite right, and looking for justification from his elders and superiors. And here was the Duke justifying in weighty terms the game he wished to play. He would be helping to save his country. It never occurred to either of them to ask why the Duke couldn't go himself. Dukes had their own purposes, their own ways. It wasn't for the likes of them to wonder about that.

Her son was gazing wide-eyed at the proceedings. He would remember this as one of the important and colourful incidents from his childhood. And Alasdair was pointing everything out to him, the Duke, the clerk, the massive castle towering high with the flag flying from the tower. He was doing this as if he were a little boy himself. Which was exactly what he was, and why she had to let him go.

The night before he left she read a section out of the Bible to him. She insisted on that. She deliberated a long time on the section she would read. Finally, she decided on the part which says: 'Put on the whole armour of righteousness'. But she knew that at best he was only half-listening. The thought that he might be killed never even entered his head. For he lived in an eternal present.

She saw this more clearly when he dressed up in his tartan, when he put on his sword. He paraded up and down, laughing heartily, and allowed young Iain to play with the ribbons on his stockings. He wanted to be off, having forgotten his home already.

As she watched him go she knew with a flash of clair-voyance (what she would call 'second sight') that she would never see him again. She wanted to shout after him, to call him back, to say that it was in her power to change herself, that she would become young again, or die. But she didn't say anything for she knew that all that was impossible. She simply took Iain's hand in hers and watched Alasdair go. He waved gaily but already he had become posthumous. She found it strange that he did not understand this himself, and followed him with her mind to tell him about it. But he turned a bend in the road, and it was as if he had stepped out of her mind as well.

She returned to the house with Iain, whose small hand was cramped in her convulsively tightening one, shut the door, and washed him.

Before she went to bed that night she read many pages of the Bible.

And six months later she received the notification and took it to the elder's house, when she had studied it. He read it and after some time said: 'I'm sorry.'

She only answered: 'He shouldn't have gone,' and then went home.

In a strange way she became rather proud of him and framed the notice. But she often wondered where he had been buried – if he had been buried at all.

In the six months she had received two letters from him. She gathered that he was enjoying himself and there were references to old Nosey: 'Old Nosey will show them.' But she couldn't understand whom he was showing what and why; and why her husband was there at all, except to escape from home. Once or twice between the lines she thought she detected some homesickness and was pleased about it. But perhaps it hadn't been there at all, and she had only wanted to believe it. Or perhaps it was true and he had found life in the army harder than he'd expected. She felt that the second of the two letters was more sober, less gay, and was sorry about that. For being who he was it was better for him to be gay.

Her own life continued. She brought up the child, sent him to school, made clothes for him, dared to speak once or twice to the schoolmaster about him. But young Iain wasn't particularly clever. He would not be a minister or a teacher.

She and Big Betty, who was older than her, became friends. Sometimes she had to borrow money from Big Betty, but always paid it back. She didn't need much money. She could exist on very little. The worst year was when they had been given the meal. After that she had learned to expect no gifts from anyone. Her sister had offered to help her with discarded clothes from the boys, but she wouldn't accept them. She hadn't been a beggar at any time during her life and she wasn't going to start now. So she knitted all Iain's clothes, jersey, trousers, stockings.

The years passed, and she almost forgot about her husband long dead in Spain.

THREE

When she rose in the morning the house at first seemed to be the same. The furniture was where it had always been. Nevertheless, she felt uneasy. It wasn't the unreal uneasiness of someone waking up in an empty house and having to summon all her objects about her in order to assure herself of her own existence by making herself superior to them. Nor was it the uneasiness of old age, the physical effort of having to get up, to put on her clothes, to hobble down with aching knees to light the fire. Yet it was a fine summer's day. The sun shone through the curtains of her window. It poured on the Bible beside her bed, turning it the colour of buttermilk. On the floor it turned to minute particles like water dancing.

She was surprised to find it was half-past nine. She didn't usually sleep so late. She dressed very slowly and lit the fire very slowly because the house wasn't cold. She made the porridge as she always did, but didn't feel like eating anything just the same. At ten o'clock young Annie came with the pails of water. Annie was a thin girl of thirteen with a thin face and thin legs. She was always cheerful, though she had a bad habit of peeing against the walls of her house while the boys usually watched her. Nevertheless she was always gay. That day she had to go to the spring of water known as the 'srup', which was about half a mile away. The well had dried up as it often did in the summer. She was an early riser and was known as the Linnet.

She came in and took some porridge, after laying the pails of water down. It was cold clear water and better than the well water. She had had to carry it up a path through the fields where the grass was all covered with dew. There was also a brae so she was quite tired.

'How are you feeling today, Mrs Scott?' she asked, swinging her thin legs about and spooning porridge into her mouth.

'I'm as usual, child,' said Mrs Scott in a preoccupied way.

'My father was talking last night. He said they had started to burn the houses,' said Annie, casually piling porridge on to her spoon in a flabby mass. 'Could I have a little more milk, please?'

'Certainly, child.'

'He says they didn't do that before. My father says he saw a shepherd. He had a stick and he couldn't speak Gaelic.'

She laughed, revealing a set of bad teeth.

'I wish the water would come back in the well,' she added. 'The cows don't have any water. I saw a cow yesterday and she had flies in her eyes.'

'Take your porridge,' said Mrs Scott, who liked to see the child eating at her table though sometimes she was wearied by her. She was wondering what clothes she herself would wear when she went out. There was a long red weal down Annie's neck as if there had been a wound a long time ago and stitches had been set in it. She was also thinking that Annie's mother should make her daughter a longer frock and one of a thicker texture. But then Sheila, Annie's mother, was not known for her house-keeping abilities though she had been in service. Annie lapped up the last of the milk and porridge and said:

'Is there anything else you want me to do?'

'No, Annie, I don't think so.'

If there was anything Mrs Scott hated more than anything else it was the indignity and helplessness of old age, having to accept favours from people, and above all her inability to pay for these favours. They did a lot for her not expecting payment. Nevertheless she knew she must be a burden to them. Here was this thin cheerful girl bringing her water every day and she had no way of paying her. She would have liked to do something for her. But she had no money to buy her a new dress. And she couldn't make one. For she couldn't thread a needle as she once used to be able to. But she liked Annie just the same for she was always bright and happy. Thinlegged, barefooted, she wasn't very clever but she was willing to help. She had a sudden idea.

'Yes, there is something,' she said.

Annie looked at her expectantly. 'It is very important and, if you do it, I'll give you a small present.' The present was a cheap little ring with only one cheap jewel remaining out of the original three. She had been given this by her father long ago. It was just a trinket, most of the glitter gone from it, except for the cheap red gem, but Annie would treasure it.

'A present?' Annie's voice seemed to rise an octave.

'Yes, a present, and I know you'll like it. But I can't give it to you till you come back. Will you do the message for me?'

'Yes.' And then, because it was true, 'I'd have done it without the present, Mrs Scott.'

Annie couldn't remember when she'd had a present last, except once when someone had sent her a pair of shoes which she still kept in a box and had long outgrown. For she never wore shoes even when she was going over rough stones and across jagged heather. She could run like the wind on her long thin legs the soles of which were as hard as leather. She felt a little guilty at accepting the present whatever it was for her mother had told her never to take anything from Mrs Scott, no matter how hard she pressed it on her. But this must be something special.

'Is it something big?' she asked tentatively. If it was big she wouldn't be able to hide it, and her brothers would take it away from her.

'No, it's not big,' said Mrs Scott in such a pre-occupied way that Annie knew she couldn't be lying.

'What is the message, Mrs Scott?'

'The message? Oh, yes, the message. Would you run along to the elder's house and ask him if he would come to see me?'

'I'm to run along to the elder's house and ask if he'll come along to see you.'

This repetition of the message served a double purpose: it sealed the transaction, and engraved the words on her memory. Annie had had difficulty with messages before. She repeated it again for good measure.

'I'm to run along to the elder's house and ask him to come and see you, Mrs Scott.'

'Yes. That's right. Tell him it's very important.'

'And I'm to say it's very important.'

'Yes. That's right. Very important. Be sure to tell him it's very important.'

'Yes, Mrs Scott, I will.'

In a flash she was off. Then she seemed to remember something.

'Thank you for the porridge, Mrs Scott.'

And she was off again.

While Mrs Scott was washing the dishes all the events came back to her, the man on the white horse, and what he had said. She recognised with a sourness in her mouth the source of her uneasiness, that her house had become insecure. Though the furniture was there it might disappear at any moment. If only her son could be at home with her. She couldn't think of anyone else who might help her except the elder. Surely he wouldn't refuse. And what had the girl said? Something about the 'burning of houses'. She had heard of this before but it hadn't seemed possible to her. She had never believed it would happen to her. Things like that happened to other people. Anyway, they just couldn't put people out of their houses, and then burn the houses down. No one had ever heard of that before. Not in the country.

She wondered vaguely what the elder would think when he got her message. Would he think she was ill? Perhaps she should have said what she wanted him for. He would hurry over thinking she was ill or dying. And the ring, she'd better get the ring.

It took her fully fifteen minutes to find the ring which had slipped inside a piece of old brown cloth. When she did find it she put it immediately in her pocket lest she should lose it again. The day was going to be a busy one for her. She would most likely have two visitors including the elder, since one of the neighbours nearly always came in.

She went to the window and looked out. Some yellow flowers, whose names she did not know, were growing outside. She didn't know the names of any flowers apart from daisies, the little ones, and the big ones one found growing near dung heaps. A little bird was pecking at the earth in front of the house. It was a sleek black, and had a bright yellow beak. She saw a woman in a long skirt hitting at a recalcitrant cow.

It was at that moment that the elder came in, accompanied by the Linnet, who shifted about in an embarrassed manner from foot to foot. She hadn't seen them coming because she was looking in the other direction. When the two of them came in she gave the ring to the Linnet, who gazed at the cheap jewel with widening eyes. After saying 'Thank you, Mrs Scott' in a high excited voice, she dashed away to be alone with her treasure. Mrs Scott watched her slow down to a more sedate pace as if she did not want to give away the fact that she had anything to be excited about. Then she sat down on the grass and began to try it on.

Mrs Scott turned away from the open door to hear the elder say:

'What did you give her?'

'Just a ring. I got it from my father a long time ago.'

She waited till the elder sat down in the chair. He had been looking at her closely and knew that she wasn't ill. He must be wondering why she had sent for him.

Mr Mackay, the elder, was a stout man with good colour in his face. The most obvious feature about him was that he had only one arm. In church he used to stand at the door and shake people by the hand with his good hand, his left. He always had a greeting for every member of the congregation. Apart from this he used to give out the reports and the magazines. Another of his duties was to place the Bible on the desk for the minister just before the minister came in. He would consult his watch and walk to the pulpit at precisely one minute before six-thirty on a Sunday night and at one minute before seven o'clock on a Wednesday night. Dressed in his navy-blue Sunday Suit he would walk up the aisle with a very slow deliberate pace, climb the steps to the pulpit and lay the big Bible on the desk. Then he would go and sit in the front pew with his wife and numerous progeny. It was said that his wife was more concerned with his position than he was. She was an incomer whom he had met when he was away sailing. You would notice when talking to her that her eyes were quite hard.

The elder sat down.

'Well, Mrs Scott, you sent for me?'

'Would you like a cup of tea, Mr Mackay?'

'No, thank you, but I would take a cup of buttermilk if you have it. I'm very fond of buttermilk. I was coming to see you anyway, Mrs Scott, strange to say. I haven't called on you now for a fortnight and it's time I did so.'

Mrs Scott hoped that later on he would offer up a short prayer, as he usually did. He liked to pray but people noticed that his prayers were becoming more and more like the minister's. He even used identical phrases.

She got him a cup of buttermilk and he drank it, savouring every drop.

'Ah, that was good,' he said, wiping his mouth. 'It's going to be a hot day. Nothing like buttermilk on a hot day.'

There was a silence.

After a while Mrs Scott began. 'A man came to see me yesterday. He was on a white horse.'

'I had heard about that,' said the elder, looking at her shrewdly. 'I heard that a man on a white horse had called. You were not the only one he called on, Mrs Scott.'

She wondered if this meant that he had called on the elder, or just on the other people of the village, or on everybody including the elder. There weren't so many people in the village anyway, only about thirty or so.

'He called on Donald Macleod,' said the elder. 'Yes, he called on him.' She didn't particularly care for Donald Macleod as he never went to church and was in the habit of saying mocking things about it. As well as that she thought he was very cocky and had a good opinion of himself. But some said he made a good job of building houses. Also, he was away in Edinburgh a lot and was fond of laying down the law to the villagers, telling them what their rights were. She dismissed him from her mind.

'Yes,' she said. 'He rode up to the house. Then he got off his horse and came in. He sat down on the bench there. He had a whip and he was beating it against the bench. Then he said, "Mrs Scott, you must leave this house".'

'He said that, did he?' The elder added, 'They do say that they are putting them out of their houses further south. It's the sheep, of course.'

'He said that. He said it was for the sheep. He said the Duke had sent him.'

'Yes.' The eyes of the elder seemed to have clouded somewhat. 'He's just a servant of the Duke.'

'That's what he said.'

Another thought came back to her.

'He said that they were going to pull down the church. I just laughed at him.'

She thought the elder would laugh too when she said that but he didn't. Her voice sharpening, she asked, 'It's not true, is it?'

'It may turn out to be the truth,' said the elder in a quiet voice, adding before she could say anything, 'We can't do anything about it. The church belongs to the Duke and—'

'The Church belongs to God,' she said equally quietly but firmly.

He looked up at her quickly. 'Well, of course, Mrs Scott, that's true in a way. Spiritually speaking, the Church does belong to God but the stone belongs to the Duke.'

He smiled with a touch of humour but she didn't smile back. She wasn't a humorous person. Alasdair had often said to her that she couldn't see a joke, that she took everything too seriously. But life was serious, wasn't it? You couldn't feed and clothe yourself on jokes.

'You see, Mrs Scott, he could send people to pull the church down stone by stone and we couldn't do anything about it. He's got the law on his side.'

'He hasn't got the law of God on his side. God would strike him dead for pulling down the church.'

The elder didn't say anything to this. He didn't even shrug his shoulders.

'Does that little girl – Annie, is it? – get your water in for you every day?'

'He wouldn't take any tea. He was a proud man.'

The elder was a little confused by this but after a while he said, 'Who? Oh, you mean the man on the white horse. Patrick Sellar.'

'Is that his name? Padruig Sellar?'

She paused and then began again:

'I thought at first that he had come about my pension.

But it wasn't that.'

'What pension, Mrs Scott?'

'The pension for my man. I never got a pension. Though I got a letter. I took the letter over to you.'

'Yes, of course. I remember now. It was a nice letter. . . How is your rheumatism these days? Do you know, Mrs Scott, that I still get pains where my arm used to be.'

What was he talking about? This was the second time he had changed the subject or had tried to.

'Ay, and he sat there and said he'd get me a new house somewhere near the sea. Think of that. What would I want to go near the sea for?'

'Did he say that? A new house, eh? Did he say what it would be like?'

'Oh, he said it would have a carpet and would be made of stone. But I told him I didn't want it.'

'Of course, of course . . . Still, a new house . . . with a carpet. That's something. Not everyone has a new house with a carpet. Why, I don't even have that myself!'

'We don't need carpets,' she said severely.

She could sense that she was being humoured and she didn't like that. Why were younger people always humouring the old? Did they not realise how annoying it was? How would they like it themselves, to be treated as if they were fools?

'I told him this was my house and I wouldn't leave,' she said firmly.

'Mind you, a new house is not to be despised,' said the elder, looking away from her. He seemed to be casting about for something to say or to be trying to find a method of approach to her.

'I see you are still managing to come to church,' he said at last. 'If only everyone was as regular as you. There's Donald Macleod now, an able man. But he won't go to church at all. We could do with another elder. He has the ability for the job.'

'They say his father wasn't like that,' said Mrs Scott.

'So I believe,' said the elder. He sighed, then smiled. 'You'll have seen my wife's new hat?'

'Yes.'

'Um. It's not easy to keep them in food and clothes. A wife and six children.'

Suddenly he got up and walked over to the window. He stood looking out.

'A new house wouldn't be bad, Mrs Scott.'

'What? Excuse me. What did you say?'

'I said,' he repeated more quickly, 'a new house wouldn't be bad.' He was still facing out and she could only see the back of his neck which seemed to her to be very red, with prickly hairs growing on it.

'I was born in this house. I spent my married life here. Now I'm old and I'll die here. I won't leave it.'

After a short silence he turned away from the window.

'Did I ever tell you, Mrs Scott, how I lost my arm?'

'I heard something about . . .'

'Well, I'll tell you. I was at sea. Not everyone knows about it. We were on this ship, you understand. And a storm blew up. Such a storm. You don't have any idea what it was like. I can't even tell you . . . We don't have any experience of storms like that here. Well, we were all running about seeing to the ropes and rigging when one of the crew was washed overboard. He had been standing just beside me when the wave took him. I heard the scream above the noise of the wind. It put a "gaoir" through my whole body. I was only twenty years old, you see.' He paused and began again: 'Well, without thinking, I dived overboard after him into the waves. I did it, you see, without thinking. I heard the scream and then dived in. I don't know how but I got hold of his hair and I kept him afloat. I was quite strong. I must have been quite strong. Well, they got a boat out but as they were getting him into the boat my arm was damaged. That was what happened to me. Of course I had to leave the sea.' He paused again, then continued: 'It's funny, you know, how as we grow older we think about things more. I don't mean we sit down and think but we have thoughts, thoughts of the future, thoughts of what might happen to us.'

He was looking out of the window as if he was seeing himself fighting through a roaring sea. 'Do you know the difference, Mrs Scott, between what I was then and what I am now?'

She didn't know what to answer.

He said: 'Well I'll tell you. I wasn't married then. That's the difference. I wasn't married then, Mrs Scott. I think a new house might be a good idea, Mrs Scott.'

'No.'

'You see, they'll put you out anyway. Who's going to stop them? They've got the law on their side. And what would you do if they put you out and didn't give you another house?'

'I don't care. I'm not leaving. I was just asking for help.'

'From a man with no arm!' The elder laughed with some bitterness. 'It's not easy, Mrs Scott, for a man with no arm, with a wife and six children.'

'It's not easy for a woman by herself with her son in a foreign land and her man dead.'

'No. No, I grant you that. But, at the same time, can't you see that you can't stop them? We would take all your furniture up and see you settled comfortably.'

'No.'

'I see.'

She tried again. 'Does it not say anything in the Bible about helping widows, Mr Mackay?'

He looked at her, half-blindly: 'No. I don't think so. I don't think there's a text about that. Not about widows.'

'There didn't need to be.' She brightened again: 'But there's a text which says, "Consider the lilies how they grow. They toil not, neither do they spin . . ."'

'Yes, there is that text,' said the elder uneasily. 'I have read that text.'

'Well, then?'

'Mrs Scott, am I going to let my children starve because there's a text in the Bible which says that you don't need to work any more than the flowers?'

His tone changed: 'Patrick Sellar came to see me.'

'I thought so.'

'He seemed a reasonable man. He said that you would have to leave but he didn't want to be brutal. He told me to come along to persuade you to go. Even before I got your message, I was going to come anyway.'

'I see.'

'Mrs Scott, I swear to you that before I came I drank a glass of whisky, a thing which I haven't done for thirty years.'

She waited.

'Why are you forcing this choice on me? I'm not strong. At one time I was strong. But not now. The future has made me afraid. I'm not a bad man. I've done my duty according to my lights.'

'You say a good prayer,' said Mrs Scott. 'Many a time your prayer at the meeting has been like water in the desert to me.'

'Well then, I tried. Won't you be reasonable? What is it you want?'

'I want someone who will help me not to leave this house.'

'Where can you find such a person?'

'I don't know.' She was suddenly weary. 'I don't know.'

'Mrs Scott, they've been burning down the houses. Do you understand that? Burning them down.'

'I think you should go back to your wife and children, Mr Mackay,' said Mrs Scott.

He wavered as if half expecting that she would ask him to say a prayer before he went. But she didn't. Her face was totally inflexible.

Did she not see how impossibly intolerant she was being? A picture returned to his mind of her handing the ring to that girl. She had said it was a ring her father had given her. So his visit must have been important to her. He made a step towards her, then checked himself. Could she not remember the near-famine many years ago? If it were to happen again what would he do? No, he could not allow his children to run that risk. And his wife. What would she say if he put himself against the face of authority. He knew very well what she would say: she too could be inflexible. To be an elder's wife was something! Yet on the other hand this woman had lost her husband. She had no one. Seventy years old and she had no one, dependent on others for even the water she drank. Trading rings for messages.

'I . . .' he began. He seemed to sway in the middle of the floor. Then, without another word, he went blindly out of the house striding, half running along, his eyes fixed on the

ground. He passed Donald Macleod who was building up a
wall near his house, and who said to him laughingly:

'Praying again, and in public too, James?'

The elder didn't even answer but continued on his way.
With a stone in his hand, Donald Macleod watched him
stride on.

'Well well,' he said to himself and then again, 'well, well,'
before putting the heavy stone on top of the others. In the
hollow from which he had lifted the stone, a lighter green
than the grass around it, he saw a snail uncoiling its black
shiny body, and covered in parts with a grey slime. Boyishly
he placed a stick in front of it to see what it would do. It
slowly drew in its horns and came to a halt and didn't go near
the stick. Perhaps God is like that, he said to himself. He
places a stick in front of us but half the time we don't sense it.
Perhaps God is a little boy like me, he thought, continuing
with his work.

FOUR

The boy was hers. She had nothing and nobody else. He toddled up to the neighbours, stood squarely planted, watched Donald Macleod build a house, sniffed the smoky thatch, smelled the tart tang of tar, or watched with fascination the hot bubbles forming themselves. Sometimes he put them in his mouth. He went up to dogs and cows and talked to them. He would sit for hours watching a cat watching him. He would sit by the cornstacks, as they were pulled down in clouds of dust, and watch the dogs racing in after the naked grey panicky mice. He would drink milk warm from the cow. He would listen to the thunder and watch the lightning. He would sit in the heat listening to the buzzing of the bees: or, with his legs swinging on a peat-bank, watch his mother building pyramids of peats. He would dangle his legs from the Druid stones which had been there from time immemorial.

And all the time she made his clothes, little woollen suits and woollen stockings. She was fighting against what her husband had told her was her weakness. She tried, at first, to make him as free as she could. When he caught a cold she didn't mollycoddle him, much as she wanted to. When later on he got into the inevitable fights in school she washed the blood and didn't scold him. Nor did she avoid speaking to the boy who had hurt him, no matter how much she wished to. For she was hoping that he would stay with her of his own free will. On one thing she was adamant. He must do his schoolwork. She went to see his schoolmaster and told him that he must keep him at it. She had great difficulty in doing this, for it was not her place to speak to a schoolmaster, especially this one who was rather sarcastic, and who instead of belting the children would pull their hair.

One day she discovered that he had been playing truant with two other boys. They had built a tent and were inside it in the stinging smoke. She dragged him home and gave him a terrible thrashing. After she had gone to bed she listened to his crying, and prayed. But she didn't refer to it in the morning. It was Mrs Macleod who had told her. She was a thin invalidish woman with a drop perpetually at her nose and an appearance of not being quite capable to cope with life. She didn't speak to Mrs Macleod for months, though at times she realised that Mrs Macleod had acted from the best of motives.

But Iain was not really very good at his lessons. He preferred to stand watching Donald Macleod at his stone-masoning and would often help him to lift some of the bigger stones into a barrow. He hardly ever read a book and was more interested in what he could touch and feel than in words. He didn't mix with the clever ones but rather with those who wouldn't attend school at all if they could help it. He made trouble for Miss Macdonald when he could, the other teacher in the two-teacher school.

He rarely was ill though he spent most of his time outside and was often drenched. Once he came home with a kitten under his jersey, hiding it, thinking that she wouldn't like to have it. She didn't, for she had no love of animals except useful ones, like cows. Horses too were useful, but not cats. The kitten died because after a while he forgot about it.

He wasn't frightened of anything much. Once he told her how, near the river, a rat had jumped straight in the air at him but he had killed it with a stone right between the eyes. He was always throwing stones, at sticks, at posts, at birds, sometimes even at horses. Once he had thrown a stone at the gurgling village idiot. She had thrashed him for that too. One of his friends had died of tuberculosis. He had gone to see him every day and stayed at the bedside, even accepting tea from the mother. In no way had he been terrified though he was not insensitive, for anyone could see that his friend was wasting away like a candle. One night he had come unafraid through a storm of lightning and thunder, and he was only ten years old. He would climb up to the roof and help with the thatching.

Sometimes he would ask about his father but didn't seem particularly interested. The only subject which interested him in school was geography. He had got a globe and would often study it. He would even tell her the names of the various countries and where they were, and enjoyed telling her. He liked the different colours used to represent the different countries. But after a short while she recognised a danger in the globe, and didn't ask him the names of any more countries. She didn't find out till afterwards that some of his fights had been caused by the fact that he was wearing woollen clothes with bright blue buttons. Such clothes were considered effeminate by the other boys. However, he never complained of this to her and sometimes helped her to thread the wool, for he had exceptionally keen eyes. He didn't like his teacher. He considered him too sarcastic and he hated sarcasm, even if it was only directed against others.

His favourite pastime was playing football. This he would do evening after evening, coming home exhausted with battered boots and dangling stockings smelling appallingly of sweat. He was very fast and was called Swifty by the other boys. When he came in with tousled hair he would go to bed and sleep like a log.

She took him to church with her every Sunday. But he was not at all interested. He preferred to be with Donald Macleod who was against the church, at least the church in their village. Eventually she stopped him from seeing Donald Macleod, but she was sure he went back just the same.

'Why does the minister smack his lips like that?' he'd say, instead of showing any interest in what the minister had actually said.

'Ministers are just like other people,' he'd say, 'they don't know any more.'

'Who told you that?'

'No one.'

'Ministers are the servants of God,' she'd say. 'And you can tell Donald Macleod that from me.'

So he grew up. He was a good worker, better than his father. He was more persistent and even defter with his hands. In fact he was very practical indeed. He would sometimes carve images of cats and hens out of wood and

paint them. She would put them on the mantelpiece though
she didn't like the practice much. It savoured of idolatry.

'Why do you do that?' she would ask him. 'God created
the cats and the hens. Why are you making them into wood?

'Because I like doing it,' was all he would answer.

As well as that he would paint the door every Spring,
spending a long time over it to get it just right. He could
thatch the house. He could plant potatoes. He could cut
peats but didn't stack them. That was a job for the women.
He could scythe the corn. He was a very good worker. As
well as that he was very friendly and got on well with people.
She knew of no one who disliked him or had a bad word for
him.

One of the things she herself disliked doing was killing
hens, which they sometimes did. The hen was put under a
creel. Iain did this with no trouble at all and the minimum of
fuss and feeling, though he wasn't cruel by nature. It was a
job that had to be done, after all. She herself didn't like to see
the hen stirring about behind the bars of the creel with its
small beady eyes looking at her. The eyes reminded her of
something which she could not call into focus and yet which
stayed at the back of her mind.

As he grew older he seemed to move further and further
away from her. It wasn't that he was doing this consciously
but she would find him sitting on the doorstep whittling at a
stick, seeming to be staring into himself. He seemed to grow
more physically awkward as well, stumbling over chairs and
altogether being an untidier presence in the house.

She never spoke to him about his father or about the army
but one night Iain asked her about him. She told him exactly
what had happened, that one day his father had gone away
and left the two of them. She told how she had brought him
up with great difficulty. She explained how she had often to
borrow money and would cry in the night because she
couldn't find a way of paying it back. She reminded him of
the long hours she had spent making suits for him. She
impressed on him her perpetual struggle, and the darkness
and hopelessness of her thoughts as she considered the
future. Feeling a profound sense of injustice she sensed that
he was becoming impatient and that his attention was wan-

dering. Would either man or boy see the serious side of the world?

'What was my father like?' he insisted.

'Your father? He didn't take anything seriously. He liked a roving life, so he joined the army. He didn't think about us.'

'He was killed in Spain, wasn't he?'

'Yes. In Spain. But he didn't care where he was going. He was just like a gipsy.'

This was the worst she could say about him. For gipsies wandered about, homeless. They lived in a world of their own and depended on others, for they were always stealing, and they frittered their time away. They had strange beliefs and wore bright clothes. They even had a language of their own. Why hadn't she thought of it before? He was really like a gipsy with his moustache, his small tanned face and his quick light movements. Perhaps, too, he believed in fortune like the gipsies. And after all they said that these gipsies came from a place like Spain.

'They live in tents, the gipsies,' said Iain idly, then later: 'He was fighting for his country, wasn't he?'

'I don't think he was fighting for anybody. He just wanted to travel. He wanted to see the world. He never sent any money home. We could have starved for all he cared. And he used to get drunk.'

But she felt that the more she talked the more, strangely enough, he admired his father. She couldn't understand it. Everything she had said was true. He wasn't serious: he didn't care for anyone but himself: he walked out on his responsibilities. He was as gay and forgetful as a child: he would have left them to starve. Nevertheless, she knew with a woman's intuition that she had made a mistake in presenting him like this to the boy. But that was how he was, she couldn't say he was any different.

'When do you think we should get the cart?' she asked to change the subject, but he wasn't to be diverted.

'None of the other boys' fathers were in Spain,' he said proudly, as if this gave him a distinction of some kind.

'Listen, Iain,' she said, laying down the jersey she was knitting. 'They stayed at home with their wives and children. They worked. They saved up for their old age. They were wiser than your father.'

'Yes, but they're all so dull apart from Donald Macleod.'

'And there's another thing. Keep away from Donald Macleod. A man who doesn't go to church is an evil man. There's no getting round it.'

'He knows about Edinburgh, about the coaches and the gaslights. He goes to Edinburgh a lot on business. He tells me about the Highland regiments. He told me about Waterloo. Did you know it was fought on a Sunday?' he said wickedly and rushed on. 'He says that Edinburgh has thousands and thousands of people in it, and that you might have sixty people living in the one building. Tenements, he calls them.'

'I told you to keep away from him,' she said furiously, her needles flashing in the light. Who did Donald Macleod think he was, with that invalid wife of his, with his news from Edinburgh, and his books? A man who didn't go to church wasn't a respectable man, no matter what way you looked at it.

'Does he speak to you about God?' she asked.

'No, he never mentions him at all,' said the boy with unconscious humour. 'He never speaks about religion. He's a good stone mason, isn't he?'

'Some people say he reads too much to be a good stone mason. You can't serve two masters.'

'Yes, he's very clever.' He said this without the slightest trace of envy and she looked at him sharply.

'Anyway, he's a bad man, not that I've spoken to him much, thank God. He shouldn't tell about these goings on in Edinburgh.'

'What goings on?'

'Never mind that. Where are you going?'

She remembered that when the first of Donald Macleod's children had died after great agony at the age of one he wouldn't allow the minister into the house. Or so she had been told. What could you expect from a man like that? 'I don't want you here with your hellfire,' he had said. 'I never sent for you and I don't want you.' Imagine saying that to the minister who had come to comfort him. The minister had

every right to be angry. And they said that Donald Macleod
had wept over the child. At least his wife had said so. But
who could believe that? If he was as sorry as that why did he
never visit the child's grave? The trouble was he read too
many books and had ideas above his station. Like the time he
had said they should form a committee to run the village.
Who was he anyway? Wanting to control everybody. And
who would be the greatest man on the committee? Wouldn't
it be himself?

Iain was washing himself in the basin, his dark head bent
over it and away from her. Through the splashings he
mumbled that he was going out. Every evening now he
dressed himself very neatly, combed his hair smoothly and
took great care over his appearance. And now he was wearing
long trousers.

Why did she always remember him best in his short
woollen trousers, his knees usually scratched and his stockings fallen to the ankles? Of course he was going to the dance
at the end of the road.

He was ready now, looking handsome and slim, hopeful
and totally defenceless. Now he was going, his boots shining
in the lamplight.

After he had left she sat there for a long time thinking, the
knitting abandoned in her lap. It was a blue jersey she was
knitting for him with a red pattern in it. She was a good
knitter: she had picked up the patterns from her mother.
Sitting there half dreaming she heard the distant music of the
melodeon. The moon would be sparkling on the water of the
river where Iain used to hunt for trout, just by the wooden
bridge. Another game they had, until she stopped Iain from
doing it after he had come home drenched, was to jump from
one side of the bank to the other, taking long leaps in their
big tackety boots. They caught the little trout with their bare
hands as they sparkled all silver in the sunshine. Now the
moon would be shining on them.

She heard a cat scream frantically in the moonlight, like a
human being in pain, and for a moment she was frightened
by it. She was nervous and easily frightened. She had seen
the nights when she would crawl inside the cupboard when
the gale was on, with thunder and lightning. During these

nights she would cover the mirrors with cloth. That was the tradition. Lightning hitting a mirror was dangerous, it could blind you. Or it could set the house on fire. She wasn't sure which.

The music of the melodeon set up strange vibrations in her. On the one hand it reminded her of her youth, on the other she didn't want Iain to be getting mixed up with girls. They weren't what they used to be, hard-working and conscientious. No, they were becoming more abandoned every day.

She went outside, attracted by the music. The moon, a huge ripe red, was low in the sky like a broody hen. Its light illuminated the whole earth so that it seemed to be as bright as day. Apart from the music there was no other sound. No, that wasn't true. There was the sound of the whooping at the eightsome reel.

Her eyes turned instinctively out to the moor, to where the Druidic stones brooded. No one knew very much about them. But they said that young children used to be sacrificed to the Druids in the olden days. They cut their throats with a knife and offered them up as sacrifices just when the sun was rising.

Once when she was young she had seen an owl seated on the edge of the moor with its big globular eyes. At least she believed she had seen it, or perhaps it had all been a dream. She had never seen an owl during the day. Owls weren't common there.

Everything apart from the music was so still, so transparent almost. She could see the cart track quite clearly and the houses whose roofs were white with moonlight.

She shook herself clear of all that and returned to the house and began to knit again. She would wait up as she always did till Iain came home. He didn't like it but she wouldn't go to bed till he returned. She had had too many vigils in her life for her to stop now.

FIVE

After the elder had gone she fell asleep. She had never been so tired in her life. She fell asleep in the chair in which she was sitting, a thing which she had never done before. For she was an early riser, always busy, idleness and unexpected sleep being almost a sin.

When she awoke the room was cold and she had to stir the fire into being again. She didn't dare to think about the elder. Some time later she would have to think what to do next but at the moment it must be one thing at a time. That was it: she must take one step and then another, testing each very carefully as if she were crossing a narrow bridge over a torrent. If only she had something to do to pass the time. But before she could think of anything Big Betty came in. Big Betty tried to call on her as often as she could, because her house was just opposite hers on the other side of the road.

Big Betty – as her name implied – was a large, ruddy-faced woman who was rather deaf and therefore tended to shout. They had had many quarrels with each other in the past, as is always the case in small villages, but now they had reached what looked like permanent amity. One of these quarrels had been about Big Betty's cow – at least a cow she used to have – which had the habit of slowly and luxuriously eating any clothes hung upon a line. Mrs Scott had lost a dress to her, and in spite of Big Betty's big booming overwhelming voice had fought her way to a draw.

Big Betty had an insatiable curiosity. If she saw a stranger walking along the road she would come out to the gate and hold him in loud conversation till she had found out everything about him she could, which, owing to her deafness, took rather a long time. She was, however, kind-hearted as many of her kind are.

'I hear the man on the white horse came to see you,' she roared. 'I saw him yesterday but I was too busy to come over.'

Betty knew all about the man on the white horse, as did all the village, but just the same she wanted to find out everything at first hand. Mrs Scott told her everything that had happened to ejaculations of 'Eh?' 'You don't say?', as well as requests to repeat what she had just said. Betty only did this when absolutely necessary – that is when reception was particularly poor and she couldn't connect the various half-heard remarks – but most of the time she refused to yield to her deafness. When she heard about the elder she professed to be scandalised.

'It's that wife of his,' she boomed. 'She wears red underclothes.'

Mrs Scott wondered vaguely how she had found out about this: perhaps her cow had been chewing again. She rather thought that the elder's wife would do better than herself in a contest with Big Betty.

'Ay, she wears the trousers in that house,' said Big Betty again.

'One lump, please. I'm getting so fat they'll soon put me between the shafts to draw the cart.'

She laughed very loudly, then stopped suddenly.

'You think of that wee Mackay. Do you think that story of his is true?'

'What story?'

'What he said happened to his arm. They all tell it different ways. Some are saying it was an accident at the mill. But you can't believe everything you hear.' She sighed. 'Six girls he's got. They should be doing something about . . .'

Seeing that Mrs Scott disapproved of such talk she added:

'You're looking tired today. What did you say? Sheep? Yes, they're saying that the whole place will be covered with sheep before many months are out. Oh, sleep. I was thinking you said "sheep". You fell asleep? Imagine wee Mackay, the elder though. But I'm not surprised about it. He always shakes hands with you at the church door and he smiles but you don't know what he's thinking. And he's always sniffing up to the minister with his wee prayers. He's only got the one prayer you know. Yes, just the one prayer. Something about "Where two or three are gathered together". He always has that bit in.'

Mrs Scott smiled in spite of herself.

'Ay, he's a trusdar right enough. I wouldn't trust him with me scarf in a gale. I like people who tell you straight what they think of you. And he doesn't look after his children all that well. He should clean their noses. And they're little pests too. I told one of them to clear off or I'd give him a good skelping.

'And see the way he takes the Bible up to the pulpit. The pride of him. I've seen the day I could have eaten him for my breakfast. Ah, those days are gone. You wouldn't think looking at me now that I could dance when I was young. But you could put a ring round my waist then. This is good tea you have here, Mrs Scott. And how are you feeling?'

'That upset me.'

'What did you say? Upset you? Upset you? Of course it upset you. Do you know, in the old days they wouldn't have come to put us out of our homes. If my father was alive he'd take his claymore to them. He was a terrible bad-tempered man, my father. Leather you as soon as look at you. But he was a good man all the same and had a good end. Ay, he died when he was eighty years old. Just dropped dead at the table. He was eating his porridge. He had the very spoon to his mouth when he fell forward upsetting the milk. He wouldn't have liked it if he had to go to his bed. Couldn't abide doctors. Sometimes they go a bit queer but my father never did, thank God. Old Mr Morrison, you know, wouldn't let the doctor into the house: he thought he was poisoning him. Ay, we don't know what will happen to us when we get old. We don't and that's a fact. Yes, I could take a bit of scone.'

She chewed decently, savouring the scone.

'What are you going to do now?' she asked at last.

'I don't know.'

'Mmm. You're keeping the house clean anyway for a woman of your age. Have you had any word from Iain?'

'I had a letter about a month ago.'

'What was he saying?'

'He's working away. But it isn't easy. The land never was any good. But he says things are getting a bit better now.'

'Uh, huh. The beggars – excuse me, Mrs Scott – are taking it out of them. That's what they're doing. Well, I suppose they'll be after us now. Do you know, that man on the white horse came to see me too?'

'Oh,' said Mrs Scott, 'and what did you say to him?'

'I didn't say anything to him. I took him by the shoulder and put him out of the house. My man was near spluttering with the nerves but I didn't listen to him. I never listen to him. I've found that is the right policy. When I heard what the wee man wanted – the likes of him – I didn't say anything, I just put him out. Of course he was shouting things: "You'll pay for this, Mrs Graham," (he knew my name too though I hadn't told it to him) and I just said to him: "You'll have to carry me out, wee man, I don't know about my man but you'll have to carry me out." And do you know, Murdina, I never saw such a face on a man. You'd think he was going to eat you up. He went as red as an apple. But I just laughed at him.

'"Do you think I'm getting a chair from Glasgow for you to put it out?" I shouted right back at him. The wee beggar. Excuse me, Mrs Scott. And there was my man trembling. Eh? I never laughed so much in my life. It did me good. He won't come back in a hurry.'

'To think Mr Mackay should have acted like that,' said Mrs Scott.

'Eh? Mr Mackay. Oh, I could have told you that myself. He's no spunk, that's what's wrong with him. Oh, you won't get any help from Mr Mackay. Is there anything you need?'

'No, thank you, Betty.'

'Mind you, when they start putting you out you'll see a lot of things you didn't imagine. You'd think Sheila was very poor, wouldn't you? Well, I can tell you that she's got a new clock in the culaisd. She didn't want me to see it but I saw it just the same. And you'd think she was poor and wouldn't wash her own underclothes, if she has any, God help me, which by the look of that daughter of hers she doesn't. Well, you'd get a turn if you saw what she's got. Ay, when they turn them all out you'll see a lot of things you wouldn't imagine.'

'They won't turn us out.'

'Eh? Did you get news from somewhere? Who told you that?'

'I won't leave. I said I wouldn't leave and I won't.'

'Ay, ay. Well do you know that daughter of Mrs Campbell? She's going to kill herself one of these nights. Thirty years old and she's walking the road at three in the morning. Do you remember Margaret? She went out and killed herself. Threw herself in the loch. You know what she needs, don't you?'

'Stop it, Betty.'

'I'm sorry, Murdina, but it's true all the same. It's a tragedy. But that's the way it is in a small village when there aren't enough husbands to go round. That was a nice drop of tea.'

'There's nothing wrong with our life here,' said Mrs Scott quietly.

'When did I say there was? We have our troubles but we have a quiet life. And we have our fun now and again. That little half-man telling us what to do. I could have kicked the backside of him. And they say there's a man higher than him.'

'There's the Duke. He said he was from the Duke.'

'I don't mean the Duke. I mean another man. But I can't mind his name just now. They say he's the chief. But he'll be away in London likely.'

'Mrs Graham, do you think if we went to the Duke . . . ?'

Mrs Graham laughed delightedly: 'The Duke? What do you think the Duke cares? He stravaigs about in front of a mirror all day. What do you think he cares? He doesn't even know we're alive. Mind you, I saw him once. He was having a look over his estates. His wife was with him on a horse. A streak of nothing she was. As thin as a stick. I'd like to have seen her with a creel. And there he was with his nose in the air and his: "How are you, my man?" And my father seventy years at the time. Well, do you know, my father took his bonnet off but he was chewing tobacco at the time and he spat it out at the Duke's feet with his shining boots. Oh, he didn't mean to – my father was a respectable man – but the Duke didn't like it though he didn't say anything. Ay, I laughed after he'd gone but my father was fair horrified. "Who are you laughing at?" he shouted. "Do you think you can laugh at the Duke? What's your generation coming to anyway?" My father wouldn't have said anything against the Duke or the Duchess. He used to call her the Lady from the Big House. He's dead now, poor soul, else I don't know what he'd say with their shepherds and their dogs and their small wee men.'

Nevertheless Mrs Scott had come to a determination though she didn't tell Big Betty what it was. There was still one hope left, at least one.

'And how are you keeping yourself, Betty?' she said.

'What am I keeping? I'm not keeping anything. Eh? How am I keeping? I'm fine, but for the rheumatics. I get it in my knee and then it shifts to my legs and then it ends up in my shoulder. But I'm not too bad, thank God. The Communions should be on us soon. You'll be going every night then?'

'I try to get out if I'm able.'

'Ay, it helps when you can get out in the air. It's not good for you to be inside so much but it can't be helped at your age. We all have to come to it. What did you think of Reverend Mason who was here last year?'

'He was a bit dry.'

'Ay, a bit dry. That's right enough. But a fine figure of a man just the same.'

'That has nothing to do with his preaching,' said Mrs Scott firmly.

'No, you're right there. He went off the text a bit, didn't he? Didn't you think that?'

'He didn't keep to the text at all. I heard the Reverend Carmichael many years ago. He used to give it to them. I remember him saying to a man once: "If you're not going to attend to me, Calum, you should go home to your rotten potatoes for I'm saying to you that in the eyes of the Lord you're just a rotten potato yourself."'

'He used to say things like that right enough. He was a strong preacher, but they said he was hard on his family.'

'He has to be hard on all sinners.'

'I suppose you're in the right there.'

'I know I'm in the right, Betty.'

'Well, you know more about ministers than I do, that's certain.' She got up. 'But I have to go just the same. My man doesn't like me to do a lot of ceilidhing. He doesn't say anything but you can tell. And he's all I've got.'

'I'll see you to the door.'

'No, you just stay where you are. Just stay where you are. I'll find my own way out.'

SIX

Inevitably there was a girl he brought to the house one night.
Elizabeth her name turned out to be. She was home for a few
days from service in Glasgow.

No, she didn't like Elizabeth. To be fair, she had tried to
like her, had at least tried not to dislike her. She was put off
by Elizabeth's red hair. What was it about red hair that she
disliked – its rarity perhaps? And her face too was pale, dead
pale, a face that had seen places that she herself had never
known and would never know, a face with hollow interesting cheekbones under the red hair. Also she was wearing
a skirt that was a trifle short. In fact she looked immodest,
alert, alive, tense. Her eyes lacked the loch calmness of the
eyes of true Highland girls. There were sudden questioning
flames to them. It wasn't the place of a girl to talk so much in
the presence of a man and an older woman. She told about
the big houses in Glasgow and the bells on the doors and the
food. She told about the river and the ships and the noise.
She talked about her gentlemen and the coaches, and pony
traps. She touched on the plate, the glass and the silver. She
herself was a parlourmaid and she told of the waistcoats and
the top hats. She never mentioned church once but she
remarked on the theatres and the gaming houses. She talked
of the hugeness of the houses, with the steps going up and
the steps going down, and how people bumped into each
other in their haste, and how no one knew anyone else. And
she talked of the parks and the gardens and the flowers and
the street-sellers. And she told of the officers and the
soldiers and the sailors and the merchants and places called
offices. And the lights at night which she called gas lamps
and their strange blueness which made your own face appear
blue. And she was very pale and there were shadows in the

hollows of her cheeks. And there was a restlessness about her.

And to all this Mrs Scott listened, but saw that she was wearing a ring when she wasn't married. And that she was wearing what seemed to be jewels in her ears. And listened to how she had saved up to come home, for she lived in the same village as Mrs Scott's sister, and Mrs Scott was thinking: I must go and see my sister about her. And didn't say very much except to suggest that there was no reason why she should have gone to Glasgow and that she had heard that Glasgow was a sink of iniquity and that no one was safe in Glasgow for they went about with knives there and would rob you as soon as look at you. At which the girl had laughed:

'Bless you, Mrs Scott, no one's ever harmed me in Glasgow,' looking down at her neat shoes.

But she had offered to wash the dishes, which offer Mrs Scott had declined. Perhaps the girl had a good heart after all but it was too early to admit it, especially – not to put too fine a point on it – when she didn't know what women her own husband had known, for wasn't it a fact of common knowledge that certain women – one could not call them ladies – followed the army and one could tell what they were doing there without too much thinking about it, and perhaps it would have been better if the girl had not mentioned soldiers at all.

And she had told the girl something about that and the girl had said how terrible it must have been when her husband went off but at the same time you could tell by her eyes that she was losing interest and Iain was looking warningly at his mother but she didn't pay too much attention to that for after all didn't he have to be saved from himself. How could this girl, so pale and fashionable, milk the cows, cut the corn with a sickle, plant potatoes, carry the peats home and do all the other jobs a woman had to do?

Unless, of course, Iain went to Glasgow.

Hadn't she done everything for him, even when her mother had been screaming inside her that she must be strict with him? And now this girl, hatched heaven knows where but quite suited to Glasgow with its lights like the fires of hell, had come to her home and was only half listening to what she had to say. And looking so confident though she was only seventeen, and casting around very likely to see if there were any mirrors in the room and comparing this house to the great houses in which she was used to staying. I do not like her, she was saying to herself, as she took back the scone which had been barely pecked at (but perhaps in Glasgow they had finer food than that and something called coffy which you could buy in a dish).

'And, Mrs Scott, I must bring you a kerchief of cotton. I think you would like it.'

'No. I have enough kerchiefs.'

Iain looked at her. The girl looked at Iain.

'I mean, I wear black kerchiefs anyway.'

What would people think of her with a cotton kerchief? This girl didn't seem to mind what people thought of her. That was one reason why she disliked her. And she didn't have to stay with the people all the year round.

'My mother means that the kerchief wouldn't be a black one,' said Iain grimly, and she could tell that he was angry. But his anger bred in her fierce delight.

'Who are you staying with?' she asked.

'With Mr Macleod. He's my uncle.'

She might have known. Who else could she have been staying with?

'He is my mother's brother,' she volunteered. 'My mother says that he was the clever one of the family.'

'He's clever right enough,' said Iain, 'and he's a good stone mason too.'

'My mother says that he's not such a good stone mason as he is a reader.'

'He's a deep thinking man,' said Iain.

But she pursed her lips and wouldn't say anything about Donald Macleod, though everyone said how he kept to himself and wouldn't go to church and had refused even to help repair it, and wouldn't cut the peats for the minister though everyone else did, and how the children liked him just the same and would help with carrying the stones and working around the houses he was building no matter how much their parents tried to keep them away. For he would tell them stories which he made up himself and not like those long dreary stories they heard at ceilidhs which bored the children. Many of them were stories about heroes who had lived long ago in far lands. But all, to Mrs Scott, represented the unfairness of existence that the children should prefer those who were corrupting them the most.

But that was enough about Donald Macleod. The devil could be charming when he liked, even when or especially when he was pulling down while pretending to build. There were too many evil stories about Donald Macleod. And hadn't he once said: 'If I were God I'd be pretty fed up of myself just now.'

This was the last straw, that she should have been a niece of Donald Macleod's. That was why she wouldn't let her wash the dishes though she did really ask to do so and was disappointed when she was refused. And she also asked questions about Iain when he was young.

'I bet he was very disobedient,' she'd say laughing.

And so Mrs Scott said that of course he wasn't disobedient. She contradicted every statement made by that little minx so that Iain's expression became blacker and blacker and yet all she was doing was praising him. Did he want it to be known that he was disobedient? And the girl's eyes became more and more puzzled as if she too had wanted him to be disobedient and, as she said, a bad boy.

Eventually she herself stayed up till the bitter end and wouldn't go to bed, though she wanted to, and the girl had gone and Iain had seen her home, or rather to Donald Macleod's, and had come back very silent and had pulled off his boots one after the other, his lips tight together, and then had gone off to bed still without saying a word though she had spoken to him not once but twice.

The following day she had gone off to her sister to see if she could find out anything about the girl who had red hair and was very lively and laughed a lot and wasn't suited to Iain at all with her talk about ships and rivers and dresses and fashions and that ring on her finger which she had no right to be wearing. She wouldn't be surprised if she went about with soldiers in Glasgow. She had heard of girls like her.

Not that she particularly liked her own sister either. Her sister after marriage had gone away and left her with the whole burden. They hadn't even had an argument about it. Her sister Jean had simply gone, turned at the door and gone. It hadn't even occurred to her that she should stay, for she had never said she was sorry for going or even seemed to think of saying she was sorry. For her sister was brisk and bright and did not suffer from the curse of suffering with others. Her sleeves were always rolled up and she was always busy and she did not hear any cries from the bedroom, except impatiently. Her sister did not think about the future nor about old age or death. Her sister could be seen in a high wind of perpetual motion, her arms bare to the elbows, working. But since she had to go and see her sister, she did.

She endured the brisk welcome and the two children – not exactly children now, one boy and one girl – and watched while her sister got rid of them briskly, saying, 'Shoo,' good-humouredly as if they were hens and they went, wherever they went to. She sat and talked to her sister, wondering curiously 'Are you happy?', whatever that meant, but she knew that she didn't need to wonder, for her sister was happy, assisted by those gods of perpetual motion, of breeze and corn, which played about her, shadowing her bare arms only very lightly with shadows that did not remain. True, she didn't look quite as fresh as before, some of the bloom had gone, but there were no signs of inner darkness. There was no sign of anything that she could see, merely that she had grown a little older and that was all. It was funny that when she had come in her sister had made a move to kiss her, then had stopped. She herself didn't believe in kissing but nevertheless she wondered what had made her sister stop, her sister who quite clearly was happy to spend her days baking and drawing water from the well and looking after her husband, who was out in the fields, and washing and sewing for her children and slapping them – when they were young, on their bottoms; when they were older, on their backs. Yet she was even able to forget about them till they came in for their meals.

She was like that; that was the only explanation for it. Either you were like that or you weren't. If you weren't there was no way of becoming like that even if you wanted to.

She herself didn't intend to stay long. She had come on a

mission and when she had finished it she would go. She hadn't come to see her sister for her sister's sake. All that was over a long time ago, on precisely the same day her sister had packed all her possessions into a trunk, had looked down briefly at her mother stranded like a fish on a rock and then had walked out of the room.

'Do you know a niece of Donald Macleod's?' she asked, refusing tea.

'Elizabeth you mean.'

'I think that's her name.'

'Yes, I know her. Why?'

'Tell me about her.'

'About Elizabeth? There isn't much. Drat that pot. Will it never boil?'

And so she had to do something about the fire, because all the time she was thinking about the pot.

'You were talking about Elizabeth. She's in service in Glasgow.'

'I know that. What else do you know about her?'

'I don't know much about her. She's young. I don't meet many of these young people.'

'You must know something about her.'

'Elizabeth? Elizabeth? She was going with a young fellow. Was it Angus Gunn? I believe it was Angus Gunn.'

'Is she still going with him?'

'I don't know. What do you want to find out for anyway? I know that she used to, that's all . . .'

'Where is he now? Is he living here yet?'

'Angus Gunn? No, I don't think so. Someone was saying he's away in Glasgow.'

'Oh? In Glasgow?' Her lips pursed with satisfaction.

'What are you "ohing" for? What's wrong if he wants to go to Glasgow?'

'I'm not saying it's wrong.'

'Will you have some tea? Are you sure you won't have any? You're acting very queer.'

'No, I won't have any. I'm not thirsty.'

'All right then. They do say she's a bit of a flirt. I wish that pot would hurry up. Well, she's a young girl. There's no harm in being a flirt.'

'Were you a flirt?'

'Not everybody is. Anyway, you couldn't call me pretty. And she's pretty. Very pretty.'

'She's too thin.'

'What?'

'She's too thin.'

'Well, well, so you've come round to talking about that now. That fire's going better. You're not going to tell me why you're asking all these questions? No? Well, you were always secretive. Anyway I have nothing against the girl.' Then, changing the subject: 'And how is Big Betty? Still as deaf as ever?'

'Yes.'

'I was sorry to hear about . . .'

'What were you sorry to hear about?'

'Nothing. It's just . . .'

'If it was about Alasdair's death you were going to speak, he was a soldier and he died for his country.'

Her sister didn't know what to do or say, that was clear. It was also clear that she wished that Mrs Scott would go away or tell her why she had come, but she wasn't going to do that. She spent another half hour with her, talking about this and that, about children and how wild they were, about her sister's husband, and how good he had been to her, about the new bed they had got because the old one which her husband had inherited had been ugly and, anyway, these beds weren't fashionable any more, about the sheep spreading north and how some people advised giving in and others advised the opposite, and as for her sister if she was sure she would get a better house to go to, a more modern one, she should go but not otherwise, and about how it wasn't easy to do anything against the law, and how Patrick Sellar and his kind always won but that she herself was more concerned with the future of her children and that you couldn't open your mouth in case there was a spy (for there were people like that, who would try and help authority in order to prevent anything happening to themselves) and how when there had been the sickness some had taken the medicine the Duchess sent but others had refused it, and some children had died because of that, and what was anyone to do, and perhaps there had even been records kept.

And that the Duchess wore the most beautiful clothes made for her in London and she, the sister, had seen her at a distance about a year or two before and that the Castle must take a lot of servants to keep up. And some girls went on service there and others had been stopped. And what could you do? If they didn't go, others would get their places and they needed the money, you couldn't argue against that. But the Castle was lovely from the outside with all those towers and lawns. And someone said that it was full of pictures inside and old swords with dried blood on them.

But Mrs Scott hadn't listened to much of that and she only stayed another half hour because that was fitting, and she always had the excuse that she had a long way to go, and that it might come on to rain. So at the end of that half hour she left her sister and as she waved to her, because that was what one did, she knew that barring accidents she would never see her again. Why should she? Her sister had left the house, she had left her to sacrifice herself. She had given her no help whatever and had never sent any money though her husband had never been idle. Well, that was the way life was, though it took some people a long time to realise it though others seemed to realise it from the beginning. If you didn't learn about it in the end you were a fool.

True, her sister had had troubles. She had nearly died over the birth of the first one, but that was a chance you had to take. She didn't think much about her sister now. She was just like anyone else to her. So she didn't really feel anything as she said goodbye to her. Nor as far as she could tell did her sister feel anything either, standing there, the breeze ruffling her frock and her arms bare as always, very like her mother in a way when her mother was young. She would just go back to the house and get the meal ready and then when she was spooning it out she'd say to her husband: 'Oh, by the way, my sister was here today'. And then they'd talk about her for a bit, but in a short while they'd have forgotten all about her. For one thing she could say about her sister, she wasn't nosey and she wouldn't worry herself about the enquiries Mrs Scott had been making about Elizabeth. That was why she had got herself such a happy life: she wasn't a worrier.

She had decided that she would go and see the minister to find out if he would help her against Patrick Sellar.

'So that's why you went to see her,' said Iain. 'All the way to see your sister to spy on a girl you hardly knew.'

'I wasn't spying. I went to find out who she was and. . .'

'You knew who she was! Are you trying to keep me in a glass case as you kept my father?'

'What are you saying? What do you know about your father?'

'I know that he ran away from you.'

He stopped and said quickly:

'You shouldn't have gone. You had no right. How would you like it if people were spying on you?'

'I was told she had a boy who went after her to Glasgow and that she flirted with everyone she saw.'

'That's a lie.'

'Go and ask your aunt if you don't believe me.'

'I don't know my aunt. And I don't believe her.'

'Have you ever known me to tell a lie?'

That stopped him again.

'Anyway, why did you think I was serious about her?'

'What did you say?'

'Nothing. I might get someone worse than her.'

'You should get someone from this village itself. Anyway you're too young for that. I was twenty-nine years old when I married. It's early enough for you to be thinking about it.'

'What would you say if I emigrated?' he said, tying his bootlaces.

'What are you saying?'

'Other boys have emigrated. I might get a better wife if I went to Canada.'

'Well, go out with Elizabeth then. I'm not stopping you.'

'Who said I wanted to go out with her? Aren't you saying she's a flirt?'

Too late she saw the trap into which he had led her. Had she brought him up too easy when she herself had been brought up too strict? The pendulum of the old grandfather clock swung from side to side. It was seven o'clock.

'Where are you going?'

'Out.'

'I'm only trying to protect you. What would you say if you found out she was a flirt after you had been serious with her?'

'Oh, I know you're only trying to help me,' he said mockingly.

'I won't say any more then. Do what you like.'

'You may have said too much.'

He had tied his laces and was standing up, his face cold and aloof. One day they were running in to have their cut knees attended to, the next they were standing looking at you as if you were a stranger. That agonised face by the bank of the river: had it seen her as a stranger? Perhaps that was true too.

'So the two of you had a good gossip and that was the end of Elizabeth?'

'No, we didn't have a good gossip. You know well enough that I don't get on well with my sister.'

'She's good enough to be a spy just the same.'

'I wasn't spying. I just asked her. Any mother would have done the same.'

'Would they? Do you think all the mothers in this village go off to their sisters to find out about girls they've seen for half an hour?'

'But – I had no one else.'

He paused, smoothing his hair, his face twitching a little. Then he continued to comb.

'Anyway it's all finished now if it ever started.'

'Finished?' she said, with a start of hope.

'You didn't expect her to come back, did you, after the way you treated her?'

'Treated her? I didn't say anything to her. I gave her tea and scones, didn't I, and I talked to her?'

'Yes.'

He seemed to be about to say something else but didn't. At that moment she was reminded of her sister coming forward to kiss her, then not doing it. He put the comb back in his pocket, leaned down lightly to look in the mirror, poised on his toes, smoothed his hair back stylishly and went to the door.

'Anyway, you can be sure I won't bring any more girls to the house.'

'I didn't tell you not to do that.'

'I'm doing it just the same. I don't want you to be setting off every day to find what your spies have to say about them. They'd find things to say about God himself.'

With which final blasphemy he went out. He nearly always whistled a tune when he was walking away from or towards the house, but not tonight.

Automatically she picked up the dirty clothes he'd shed, the dungarees caked with mud, the jersey with the dominant knitted pattern at the waist, the thick stockings smelling of sweat, the dull muddy boots. She cleaned what could be cleaned and then put them away. In the silence she heard a cock crowing. That was a bad sign, to hear a cock crowing at night. One should only hear them in the morning.

'What have I done wrong?' she asked herself.

She took out the Bible, turned to the part where the Ten Commandments were and read them over and over, especially the sentences which said 'Honour thy father and mother'. She had certainly done that but he wasn't doing it. All the time she was reading she was thinking about the parts of the Bible like the Prodigal Son, and David crying over his son: 'Oh Absalom, my son, my son, Absalom.' But the commandments were the important parts. They came from God himself and told man what he must do. He must keep the Sabbath, worship no graven images, and honour his parents, 'that his days might be long in the land which the Lord his God had given him'.

She didn't like that talk about emigrating. That was something new. He had never talked about it before. 'I was only doing my best,' she said aloud. 'I was only protecting him. It isn't easy for a woman to rear a boy. It's easier when it's a girl.' She was slowly filling with anger, like a well, when she saw in front of her mind her husband going off gaily to the war. She knew now as then that he was taking the easy way out. For there are other dangers than those of the sword and the gun, and wounds deeper than those dealt by these. War is simple: you kill or are killed: you stay or run away. But you couldn't run away from a growing boy, who didn't know when his mother was trying to help him.

O, mother, mother, perhaps you could have told me what was best, if you still lived. When I listened for your scream in the dark I had no time to think of anything else. Life was simpler then. I had an enemy to fight and its name was death. Now I don't know what I'm fighting. But I must try to do the right thing and I did it. I found out what she was like and I told him. But like his father he would not face the truth. That was why he went out. He was running away, exactly like his father. Mother, mother, when you couldn't see me though you were looking at me, when you thought of me – if you thought at all – as a stranger or a stone, even then I relied on you. I knew you would always do the best thing and think the right thing. You wouldn't want him to marry that trollop, would you? If you could only speak reasonably and not scream and be as you once were when I clutched your skirts as the dog barked and the big bull roared and the crow dived out of the sky at the little fluffy yellow chickens. Mother, I must go on without you but I will always do what is right since you taught it to me.

NINE

The day she went to see the minister she dressed as carefully as she could. It was a long way to go and she was very nervous. She hardly got any sleep the night before, wondering what she would say and how she would act, for he had a big house and servants. It might be that when the moment came she wouldn't be able to say anything at all. She might just stand there completely tongue-tied: for it wasn't an easy thing to speak to the minister. In fact she had never spoken to him before. True, he might say 'Good day' to her but there had never been any conversation. The minister had a lot on his mind.

That night she thought about him and didn't sleep well. He was a big burly man who kept himself to himself in the huge manse. Apart from being the minister he was said to be clever and to write little books. She didn't much approve of this for she didn't think it was a minister's job to be clever. After all, hadn't Paul said that to be a Christian you didn't need to be clever? But she had to admit that he made a good sermon, though now and again he was inclined to show his cleverness and explain how certain words could have different meanings. This only confused her but he could get a lot out of a text. She remembered a particularly good sermon on the text 'I will arise now and go to my father' in which he had shown that the father of the Prodigal Son was meant to be God. This text had made a strong impression on her for he might have been speaking of her son who had gone to Canada. She often thought that he was speaking to her personally.

So all that night she was thinking of what she would say and do and was tired when the morning came, beautiful and innocent and calm with its bluish mist concealing the power of the sun. She could hardly eat anything and her stomach seemed to have gone to her mouth. But she did manage to cram something down. It would be better for her to go in the morning because she was at her strongest and best then and she was sure he would be at home. If she waited till the afternoon she might change her mind. There was no way of locking the door and she wouldn't have dreamed of doing so anyway. No one ever locked a door in the village, no matter how long he or she was away from the house. There was nothing to steal and anyway no one stole. She could not remember anybody stealing anything and if anyone did he wouldn't last long in the village. For stealing was a great crime. Who could hold up his head again if he stole anything?

She walked slowly along the road not meeting anybody at first for they would be out at the corn. In the distance she saw the sun flashing on silver. It would be a sickle or a scythe. However, she was not destined to reach the minister's house unaccosted. At the very end of the road she saw Mrs Macleod stacking peats near the fence. She didn't particularly care for Mrs Macleod but at the same time she couldn't pass her without speaking.

'Why, Mrs Scott, what a surprise.'

She couldn't think of anything to say but: 'It's a fine morning.'

'It's that indeed,' said Mrs Macleod coming towards her, carrying a peat in her hand almost absentmindedly. Her dark eyes were glinting, curious to know why Mrs Scott dressed in her Sunday black was walking along the road at that hour. But she didn't ask directly.

'You get a lot of dust on the road in summer,' she said, looking at the long black skirt.

The road was blinding white and pitted with holes, now dry and dusty. Mrs Scott walked on the grassy verge of the road by the ditch in which there was a little water, green and slimy.

'You wouldn't like to come in for a minute?' asked Mrs Macleod.

'No, thank you just the same,' said Mrs Scott.

All around her the air was fresh and new. She hadn't been out as far as this for a long time. She pulled her hood down over her brow. Said Mrs Macleod:

'I hear you had the man on the white horse to see you.'

'Yes, I had that,' she said.

'Ay, he was in most of the houses.'

There was a silence, Mrs Macleod finally breaking it in a worried manner:

'You never know what will happen do you?'

'No.' No indeed.

The house at the back seemed unusually quiet. There wasn't much water in the barrel at the door. A few hens scrabbled in the dust. A cock suddenly raised its head and crowed for no reason. Her husband must be away again in Edinburgh, thought Mrs Scott. He didn't seem to look after his own house though. There was no look of fresh paint about and the door was cracked and starving for paint.

'It's worrying, isn't it?' said Mrs Macleod, looking at her in a scattered way. But she looked worried too, as if she would cry any minute. She was supposed to be really helpless in outside work.

'I don't know what to do if they put us out,' she said. 'With so many children.'

Mrs Scott wasn't feeling very tolerant that morning. It was the same for everyone, wasn't it, and anyway Mrs Macleod had a husband she could rely on. She was sure that Donald Macleod would be all right. He was the sort of man Patrick Sellar would like, a man who wasn't interested in the church and spent most of his time in Edinburgh. In fact he might help Sellar to pull the church down. It was the sort of thing he would do, laughing and making jokes.

Mrs Macleod looked as if she was about to say something else but didn't. She looked down helplessly at the peat in her hand as if she had just noticed it, then hearing the crying of children said quietly:

'Well, I suppose I must get back. I have the dinner to make. Be careful when you're crossing the bridge. They say it's not very steady.'

Mrs Scott said nothing and walked on till she came to the river where the wooden bridge was. There was still some water in the river but she didn't look at it much for it would dazzle her eyes with the sun flashing on it like that. There was no hand rail and though it was a reasonable width the

bridge seemed to have rotted and was swaying a bit. One of
the planks had a hole in it and all of them were slimy. She
managed to cross, breathless and frightened, keeping her
eyes away from the water and looking only at the wood of the
bridge. Below her she knew there would be little darting
trout but she had no time for that. She reached the other
side, her shoes sinking in the dampness, and stopped for a
little time, collecting herself again. Then she set off across
the moor, red with heather. She found herself thinking of the
days when as children they used to go out and collect the
purple blaeberries into jars. For hours they moved from
clump of heather to clump of heather, heading northward all
the time, their mouths becoming more and more purple: and
they jumped peatbanks under the great bowl of the sky till
finally they lost sight of the village altogether and were in a
strange new world without boundaries, crawling along, filling the jars.

Steadily she tramped on, some yellow flowers fluttering
slightly at her feet. A lark flew up startled in front of her and
climbed into the sky twittering. She didn't look up. Once she
was startled by the whirr of a larger bird, like a clock being
wound up. No animal, however, moved around her, no hare
and no rabbit. Up above her, though she didn't see it, a crow
was hanging. Once a wasp sped angrily past her face and she
flicked at it with her hand. Bees were humming round the
heather flowers. In the old days she would have looked for
white heather.

Seen from above she was a diminutive figure in black
plodding steadily across the moor alive with yellow and
wine-red, her shoes sinking into the moist earth. To the
south of her there rose gently lazy smoke from the village, a
thin blue into a bluer sky. In the distance she could hear
someone hammering, perhaps repairing a fence. But she was
alone on the moor. Not quite alone, for she came suddenly
upon an object which at first she took to be a piece of dirty
cloth. As she approached it she could hear a thick buzzing
sound which puzzled her, a buzzing as of a great number of
flies, almost like the sound of a sleepy saw sawing fresh
wood. When she came to the object she looked down and
almost turned away with disgust and sickness. It was the

carcass of a thin sheep, soiled white with a black head, one of the Highland sheep of which people owned one or two. But nevertheless she stayed there for a while, fascinated with feelings of revulsion and pity. The sheep stared up at her, both its sockets empty and yet liquid as if with tears. The crows could have done that and indeed as she looked she saw a crow some yards off, staring at her stonily with fixed eyes as if there was real intelligence behind them. There was a gash in the sheep's side at which the flies were buzzing in a domestic sort of way. In fact it all looked very homely. The buzzing reminded her of the humming of Sunday pots on boil. All the living beings she could see – which were the flies – were busy, all except the sheep whose black legs were twisted under it and the crow which was waiting for her to go, as if it had staked a claim to the place. Now that she could see it more clearly she noticed that its thin black head was twisted on its neck at an unnatural angle. It was quite quite dead and yet in a disturbing way it seemed to be appealing to her out of its empty sockets. The flies of course didn't notice she was there. They hummed fatly and richly at the wound.

She stared at them for a long time, then continued towards the manse. The crow stayed there till the last moment, then with an angry 'caw' rose into the air, flapping its wings and gently hovering till she had gone. After that it would return to the sheep again. Already it had picked the eyes out cleanly like gems from an old brooch. She hated crows for they used to swoop and take the chickens from the ground. She had lost many chickens that way, as well as to the gales which lifted them up and blew them towards the moor. She looked back but the crow had settled again, still a yard or two from the sheep. She continued walking, deliberately avoiding the lochside where her mother had once screamed on a moonlit night long ago. She could see the sun dazzling among the reeds and the blue of the water but she kept a good distance from it. There wasn't long to go now.

When she came to the manse the first thing she noticed was the garden. Villagers, of course, didn't have gardens and in general didn't think of flowers as things which had to be nursed into existence and considered in an aesthetic way. In fact they didn't think of them at all as separate from the earth

in which they grew. To plant and cosset flowers into existence would be considered an effeminate and silly activity.
You couldn't eat flowers; and as for beauty – what was that?
Nevertheless, she stopped and stared at the flowers, which
were all different colours from red to purple. She saw a green
plant writhing its way up one wall of the manse. She had
never seen ivy before.

'Good day, Mrs Scott.'

She turned and there was Mr Macmillan coming towards
the minister's peatstack with a wheelbarrow. All gathering of
peats and planting of potatoes and practically everything else
was done for the minister by the villagers.

Mr Macmillan had an old bedridden sister who had been
ill for years and whom he looked after with an almost
womanly tenderness. He was a very religious man but would
not become an elder because he didn't think himself worthy
of such a position. Most days you could see him working at
the quarry, carrying stones about endlessly in a wheelbarrow, and covered with white dust. In fact, you couldn't think
of him apart from his wheelbarrow, bent over it as if he had
been born with one in his hands and was pushing it towards a
horizon which he would never reach. He was always working
except when you would see him spitting on his hands to
make the wooden handles of the barrow softer, or when he
was eating a piece of bread sitting by himself on a gravelly
slope above the quarry.

'And how are you keeping, Mrs Scott?' he shouted
without halting in his stride, as he made towards the stack to
tip the wheelbarrow over.

'Not too bad, Mr Macmillan.'

'I am glad to hear it. Just pull that rope.'

And he was absorbed in his work again.

She went up the stony path and pulled the rope at the
door, causing a bell to jangle in the hollowness inside, so
great a noise indeed that she was frightened that she had
pulled it too hard. Written in front of her on a door more
massive than any she had ever encountered were the letters,
in gold, STRATHNAVER MANSE. The bell's jangle seemed to
prolong itself indefinitely till finally, as it was fading away in
short irresolute waves, a young girl wearing a black apron

and a white pinafore came to the door, opened it and looked at her in some surprise. She didn't recognise the girl and thought that possibly she might be one of the minister's relatives.

'Is it the minister you want to see?' the girl asked in a kind of impudent tone to which Mrs Scott was not used.

'If the minister would see me for a minute,' she heard herself saying. Behind her she could hear Mr Macmillan humming a psalm tune as he worked at the peats, and this comforted her.

'I'll see if he will speak to you,' said the girl, turning on her heel and leaving her at the door.

Mrs Scott felt a vague unease stir in her, like a snail under a cold stone. She didn't know what she had expected. Perhaps to find the minister himself come to the door and draw her inside in a kind manner. But the impersonal nature of this encounter frightened her a little. She found herself staring through the open door into a hall and saw directly above her a deer's head nailed to the wood, the eyes glassy under the spreading antlers. Behind it a stairway rose, darkly spiralling, and on the curving wall could be seen a portrait of a minister in dark robes. She couldn't see the face, however, and was trying to make it out when the girl returned to say:

'Follow me, please.'

She followed her down the hallway till they came to a door. The girl knocked and the minister said 'Come in' and she found herself in a room with tall windows and shelves crammed with books. She had never thought the whole world could contain so many books.

The minister was sitting at a tall desk. She had evidently interrupted him in his writing – perhaps Sunday's sermon. Rays of sunlight fell across the desk, catching in a mesh the huge Bible he had been consulting. She didn't know what she ought to say or do. The girl had gone but the door remained open.

'Would you please shut the door?' said the minister, coming from behind his desk and standing in front of the fire, quite a large one even though it was a fine day. On the mantelpiece were glass ornaments, some in the shape of animals though she didn't know their names. She shut the door.

'Have a seat Mrs . . . Macleod, isn't it?'

'Mrs Scott,' she got out.

'Oh, of course, Mrs Scott. Such an inexcusable mistake.'

She sat down, very delicately, her hands folded in her lap.

'And now,' he said, gathering the skirts of his long coat behind him, 'what can I do for you, Mrs Scott? I trust that you are well?'

'Yes, thank the minister. I hope the minister is well himself.'

'Oh, I am quite well, Mrs Scott, thank you, quite well. But I must say that I have a lot of cares these days, Mrs Scott, and many responsibilities. To win over souls to the Lord is a wearying task, Mrs Scott.'

She was aware that he was looking at her keenly while his mouth was speaking these words.

'And what is it, Mrs Scott, that you came about exactly?' The clock on the mantelpiece struck sharply, startling her for a moment and seeming to add urgency to the minister's words. At the same time he went and sat down at the desk, looking at her over it as she had once seen the schoolmaster do when she had gone to ask how Iain was getting on with his lessons. She had to pull the chair round a little to face him. His head was caught in the light, the Roman nose, the face which was still plump without being round, the full lips, which were very red, the fine forehead under the fringe of grey hair. She didn't know how to start, and was aware that his fingers were tapping restlessly on the desk in front of him.

'I came to see the minister about the man on the white horse.'

'Man on a white horse?' he echoed richly, leaning back in his chair, his hands folded across his stomach.

'Yes. He came two days ago. He said he was going to put me out.'

She thought his eyes narrowed slightly.

'Oh, you mean Patrick Sellar?'

'The minister will know his name better than me,' she said, and was surprised to see his blue eyes flash a little before he smiled again.

'Let me get this clear,' he said, leaning forward. 'You came to see me about Patrick Sellar who came to your house and said he was going to put you out?'

He walked over to the fireplace and stood there, legs straddled. She had to turn round in the chair again.

'Well, Mrs Scott,' he said good-humouredly, 'and what do you want me to do about it?'

She looked down at the floor and then at the fire which she could see between his legs.

'I was thinking . . . that the minister might write . . . might write to tell him that . . .' She stopped.

'To tell him what, Mrs Scott?'

Irrationally she said:

'He was saying that they were going to pull down the church.'

'Yes, Mrs Scott. That is perfectly true.'

Something was going on in her head, though she couldn't tell what it was. The strange surroundings and the tension of going to see and speak to the minister in his own manse, the sunlight and the fire were having an effect on her. She swayed a little.

'Are you all right, Mrs Scott?'

'Yes,' she said, gritting her teeth. 'I am all right, thank the minister.'

'I'm glad of that. I was going to say that they are going to build another church in the north. I had a long discussion with Mr Sellar about it.'

He frowned, placed the tips of his fingers together and said:

'Have you ever thought, Mrs Scott, that this is a visitation?'

Still looking at her he clicked his fingers sharply, then continued with some anger:

'I mean that the people of this village, aye, the people of all the villages here, have deserved this. Have you ever thought that this came as a punishment for their sins?'

He walked over to the window and she followed him with her eyes. 'Looking out into the bright light of summer, Mrs Scott, seeing the birds of the air and the flowers of the field it is not easy to remember and remind ourselves of our sins. It is not easy to remember those things that we ought not to have done, and the things that we ought to have done but haven't. Night after night I hear them dancing, Mrs Scott. Sometimes I cannot get on with my work because of it. Oh, I have spoken to them about it, but the young are not so responsible as they were – and whom must we blame but their elders?'

As he ceased to speak Mrs Scott sank into a daze at this new view of things. Was it perhaps true that Patrick Sellar, the man on the white horse, had been sent as their scourge? Was he a penance imposed by God Himself?

'I have served here for many years as the servant of God's servants,' the minister said, standing at the window, his beautiful resonant voice filling the room, his handsome head haloed with sunlight. 'And I can tell you of practices that a daughter of God would not believe.' He nodded his head emphatically three times. 'I speak of their carnality, Mrs Scott, and their music which is not the music of David. I speak of some who do not attend church at all. I speak of a growing lawlessness amongst my flock. I speak of a general lawlessness in the whole land. How many of them come to the tables of the Lord? How many of them are not thinking of the flesh and their worldly pleasures? How many of them are learning disobedience to their lawful master the Duke? Why, I have heard of some who refuse to serve in his army.'

For a moment, entranced by the thrilling voice, Mrs Scott was nodding her head in agreement with what he had to say. It was true enough, what he was saying. Some of the words struck home to her, buried themselves in her heart. The music was ungodly, the young were disobedient, the world was changing, there was much lawlessness. Sin, all in scarlet, was striding the world like the huge soft round red flowers in the minister's garden. But when the minister began to speak about the Duke, and added:

'Do you know that when the Duke was asking them to join his regiment – to fight for their lawful king and country – not one of them volunteered?' the spell was snapped, she raised her head and looked up directly into the light. The minister, sensing that he had made a mistake, continued as if he hadn't noticed.

'Not that that is the important matter. What is important is the attitude it shows. Where one is not loyal to one's earthly master one is not likely to be loyal to one's God. Didn't the Lord Himself say that we must be loyal to our earthly masters?'

He stopped, then said in a different tone:

'It is their land, Mrs Scott, and the law is on their side.'

'Does the minister think that it is right for them to put me out?' she said daringly, squinting into the light where the head was golden.

'Mrs Scott, we are all going to be put out. I myself am going to be put out. I shall have to leave this manse which I have loved and this church which I have built with my own hands. Do you not think I will miss them though I have had to suffer much obduracy?'

Why had he said he had built the church with his own hands, which he hadn't done?

'Mrs Scott, I had a long talk with Mr Sellar. He struck me as a reasonable man, a man who must carry out his orders, albeit a man who will show humanity to the weak. I say I had a long talk with him. He promised us all houses, aye, better houses than we have at present. He told me of a place where you would all have a second chance, a chance to begin anew. Mrs Scott, do you know, can you imagine, what it is to be able to begin again? To have a second chance? How few of us in this world, Mrs Scott, are given a second chance.'

Again the words struck home. Did she too not need a second chance? Could she begin again, miraculously transformed, be neither too hard nor too soft, learn to love and be loved, escape the voices screaming out of the darkness?

'No, Mrs Scott, they are not monsters. They are reasonable men.'

Patrick Sellar a reasonable man? The minister was sitting behind his desk again watching her, his little eyes seeming to twinkle. And perhaps because of the eyes, which remained cold though they appeared to twinkle, or a trick of the light, or the way his head was cocked, or was it perhaps because of the buzzing of a fly on the windowpane, she was reminded of the crow which had stared unwinkingly at her, only rising at the last moment, as she had left the dead and dreadfully wounded sheep behind. The buzzing of the flies seemed still to be at her ears.

'Do not believe, Mrs Scott, that I do not see your diffi-culty. Nevertheless, I'm sure you will be helped to remove your furniture and . . . er . . . impedimenta. I'm sure that Mr Sellar will see to that.'

'The minister. . .' She began as he came over as if to take her by the arm and lead her out. She was about to say 'The minister knows best' but the words stuck in her throat. She only managed to get out the two words 'The minister' before she found herself being thrust towards the door, the darkness in the hall blinding and chilling her.

'And I am sure we will see you in church this Lord's Day as usual,' said the minister startlingly. She almost caught a weakness in the voice. Eyes bent on the ground to find her way, she did not answer. Something was causing her to shudder, spasms of cold and fear were shaking her internal-ly. When she reached the door she turned away from the blinding light, which rose straight at her face like a huge white door opening.

'You are quite all right then, Mrs Scott?' said the minister with a false tenderness in his voice, his hand on the door, to his right the red shine and fat glitter of garden flowers and behind him the mazy winding of the ivy like a long green snake clutching and weaving. Mr Macmillan was not to be seen. Endlessly cheerful, endlessly industrious, he would be away with the barrow and loading it with another burden of peats.

Leaving the manse she felt completely desolate. She heard the door shut behind her. The heady scent of the flowers was in her nostrils, like an obscene perfume. A picture of her mother stepped into her mind as if straight from a garish frame and stabbed her like a knife. Inside the barred creel she saw the caged bony face moving to and fro. She found herself half-running, having covered a good distance already. It was much hotter now and her hands were prickly with sweat. Ahead of her the ground seemed to be heaving and the air full of smoke and fire. Panic seized her. She wanted to be home. 'I must get home,' she thought, as if the house had disappeared in her absence. She had a dreadful fear that she was going to die on the moor like the sheep she had seen. She steadied herself and took another step into the sun. On and on she walked, following old paths impressed into her brain.

This must have been why when she passed by the loch she stopped and looked at it and at the reeds growing out of it. Midges were moving on the surface of the water in a thin cloud. The loch looked innocent, gentle, calm, without a tremor. This apparent tranquillity belied its depth. She looked at it, thinking of that night many years before. She saw again the twisted face sparking hate at her between bars of moonlight – not, she hoped, recognising her – and she heard again the obscenities that poured out of the toothless mouth.

Staggering, she left the lochside and made her way across the moor. This time she didn't pass the sheep, nor did she see any crows. All she was set on doing was getting home. After that she would think again. With her head bent she noticed more and more living things among the heath and grass. An insect winged with light was fluttering about before her. She saw some ants and again something slithered quickly away with an eel-like motion through the crackling heather which was coloured a living blood red. A bee swung upside down on a yellow flower, palpitating. She came to the river and the bridge. Head bent, she saw small trout flashing deliriously in the sun, sparkling in spots of blinding white. What was that in the water? A jersey, a pair of woollen pants? A child's face smiling up at her slightly distorted? She leaned down to see more closely and fell into the sparkling water, what there was of it.

TEN

The SS *Hope* lay at anchor in the bay, her sails rippled by a dull breeze. Mrs Scott was standing beside Iain. Seated on the ground a drunk man was singing to himself and cradling a bottle to gipsy cheeks, prominent and inflamed. A piper, his hands fingering the drones, was walking up and down not playing, in a proud corner all by himself, a plaid of red and green over his shoulder. There were a number of other people, less easily individualised, as well as Iain who, dressed in his navy-blue suit, was sitting on his trunk trying not to look nervous. Or perhaps he wasn't nervous.

There had been stories about these ships, of their going off-course, of taking two or three months more than they should because of gales which they were unfitted to encounter, of outbreaks of dysentery because of bad food, of people herded together as tight as sardines, of emigrants being promised good work and having to fell trees and cultivate stony land at low rates of pay, of some being abandoned altogether, of exiles dying of exposure, of heart-break and fear, of heartless agents, of, in short . . . despair.

The drunk was singing to himself the words of a Gaelic song.

An Quebec chaidh mi air tìr 's thug mi sgrìob feadh an àit.

(At Quebec I went ashore and I took a walk through the place.)

Fearann cragach agus chraobh, chan 'eil fraoch ann ri fàs.

(Stony land, and trees, there is no heather growing there.)

One of the women who was with her husband was whispering something to him while looking disgustedly at the drunk. He patted her hand and whispered, as if he were telling her there was no harm in him. And indeed there wasn't, for he seemed to be lost in a dream of his own. Mrs Scott, too, was disgusted at the drunk.

'Mind you keep away from him,' she said to Iain. The time had passed for her to persuade him to stay.

'I can look after myself,' he replied, smiling in that defenceless way of his. Soon the boats would be coming to take the emigrants out to the ship, which was riding with white sails on the grey metallic water, crinkled like the face of an old woman. It was going to be hard for her to return to her house tonight, Mrs Scott was thinking. The drunk got up and did a little dance, quite spontaneously, looking at them defiantly when he had finished, then sat down again just as suddenly, his head on his breast. He stopped singing, his head swaying to and fro, his unshaven bluish face making him look like a tramp. The others kept away from him. Suddenly the piper began to pace purposefully up and down, his plaid flying about him in the breeze, tuning his pipes. The first boat came towards the shore. Iain made as if to rise but she kept him back, down on the trunk.

'And make sure that you wear that new jersey,' she said. 'They say that Canada is a very cold place.'

He smiled.

'And change your socks after you've been working hard.'

'Yes, mother.'

'And read the Bible I gave you. Make sure you do that. And pray.'

His eyes were on the boat into which people were clambering. The piper had now gone down to the shore and was playing a tune of farewell, his fingers slowly locking and unlocking the holes in the chanter. He looked proud and private as if set apart in a world of his own, of which he was very conscious, his cheeks puffed out, his bearing martial and erect.

'Write as often as you can,' she was saying, her black hood stirred by the breeze.

'Are you sure you've put all your stockings in?'

'Yes, mother.'

To their right a woman was crying. The first boat was

now heading back towards the ship. Some object had fallen out and the sailors were fishing at it with an oar. The drunk had wakened up and was walking up and down behind the piper, parodying him and doing little skips in between, his cheeks puffed up and his hands on his chest as if he were playing a chanter. A child giggled. This pleased the drunk who continued to pace up and down more energetically. Finally, as an inspired gesture, he put the neck of the bottle in his mouth and tapped on it with his fingers as if he were playing. A drop or two which had been left at the bottom dripped out of the bottle. Mrs Scott gazed at him with distaste but was not surprised to see that Iain was laughing.

'And make sure that you make decent friends,' she whispered. 'And look after your money. And don't go spending it on drink, whatever you do.'

The piper took no notice of the drunk parading up and down behind him like a distorted shadow. Perhaps he hadn't even seen him, immersed as he was in his own dignified, complicated music. Across the water sounded the elegiac notes and from the ship came the first faint fluttering of handkerchiefs. The drunkard came to a halt and waved back with a dirty scarf. He suddenly offered the last oozings of his bottle to a tall dignified looking man with a drip at the end of his nose. But the man turned away.

'Ah well,' the drunk said to the crowd. 'Farewell. . .' And he began to sing again as he went down to the place where the boat from the ship would be coming in.

Far an d'fhuair mi m'àrach òg. . .
(Where I was reared when I was young.)

Then, his mouth open, he slumped to the ground and fell asleep. The piper played on, ignoring everything and everybody around him, but by this time he was standing absolutely still. The boat came and went. At last, Iain had to go. Mrs Scott's face crumpled, but she didn't cry.

'And make sure that you eat your food,' she said.

He bent and kissed her and turned to go. As he did so she took out of her pocket her father's gold watch and put it in his breast pocket.

'Take it with you,' she said. 'It will keep good time for you.'

He looked at her as if in surprise, then put his hand on the pocket where the watch was. He turned at the shore and waved, then climbed briskly into the boat, sitting there with his back to her. She put her hand over her mouth but didn't cry. One of the sailors was saying something to Iain but she couldn't hear what he answered.

It was the last boat and as it reached the ship the piper suddenly stopped playing. There was a great silence. As if awakened from a dream she looked around her and saw the dozen or so people left, all women and children. The piper began to put his pipes away. Without thinking, as she watched the ship, the wind stirring its sails, and watched the loch and seagulls swooping low over it, she began to sing the Old Hundredth:

> Togadh gach tir àrd-iolach glaoidh
> do Dhia Iehobhah mór.
> Thigibh is dèanaibh seirbhis ait
> 'na làthairsan le ceòl.

Through blinding tears she heard the tune being raised by the other women. The piper was standing stiffly at attention on the shore. She stopped singing because her voice was beginning to crack, and it was only then that she heard the answering voices floating across the water, the two groups – those on the ship and those on shore – united across water by the psalm, amongst the best-loved and gravest of all Gaelic psalms. Seagulls wove edgy patterns across the psalm, and behind it too one could hear the restless movement of the water as it flowed to and from the beach. When it was ended they all, as if by instinct, turned away in the direction of home. She kept a little behind, wishing to be by herself. She always believed in keeping her griefs private. That night was the worst in her life. To come to the door and know that she would find no one: to see a house completely empty. It was like coming to her tomb while she was still alive.

When she entered the house she went down on her knees and prayed. She wept and prayed for what seemed years. After that she walked aimlessly about the house, opening and shutting drawers. She took out the Bible and read chapter after chapter aloud as if it were some kind of drug, and always in front of her flickered the white wings of the ship like an angel which concealed in its holds a devilish plague.

She saw Iain sitting in the boat. He was sailing away, and in spite of everything he was happy. That was the worst thing of all to bear, if there was anything more she could bear. Big Betty came in and said:

'I was making some scones anyway. . .'

So it all began again.

ELEVEN

She could tell she wasn't in her own bed. She could tell this because she didn't seem to be facing in the right direction. As well as this the pillows were very high. In the distance she could hear a number of voices, faint, as if talking through water. The room was cool and dark like her own room, though she knew it wasn't her room.

She opened her eyes slowly, carefully. There was something on her head, a tight cloth of some kind. She didn't want to move but, perfectly still, watched through half-closed eyes the white-washed wall in front of her. She had never seen it before. In the high corner between the wall and the ceiling slightly to her left there was a spider's web, but she couldn't see any spider. She watched it but no flies appeared either. It was a delicate structure swaying outwards from the rings at the centre. She was quite content to watch it and the whitewashed wall. She had no desire to move, and sensed that if she did she would be in discomfort. Outside, she heard a cow mooing, then a child shouting. Someone spoke and the child was immediately silent. She wished they hadn't told it to be quiet, whoever they were. She closed her eyes again. When she opened them particles of sunlight were dancing on the wall, like water sparkling. They flickered gaily and seemed to flare up and then go out. This puzzled her but she just watched their flickering. This time she slowly moved her head, feeling the band over it. In front of her eyes was a window set in the wall with curtains across it. The curtains were stirring in the breeze. That was why the sunlight flickered and seemed to go out. The curtains were billowing out slightly, allowing the sunlight in and afterwards shutting and locking it off.

She let her gaze travel through the window between the

curtains when they opened. In the distance she could see vague blue hills. Then the curtains swelled again and shut them off. The curtains had flowers on them, all different colours. They billowed outwards, then stiffened inwards in the breeze. There was no other movement. The house seemed completely silent, as if it were a Sunday. She could tell it wasn't the silence of emptiness. It was a silence of hushed voices. It was a full silence, a silence of secretiveness, a silence of hidden flurries like a stream. A stream. What was it about a stream? She turned away from that. There was a tall bed-board at the foot of the bed. Sunlight flickered on it also, a minute sea of little dots. Slowly, carefully, she stretched her legs and touched the board with them. The sunlight flickered more quickly now. She closed her eyes and slept.

TWELVE

When she opened her eyes again it was growing dusk. She couldn't see through the window and the whitewashed wall had darkened, had become thicker as it seemed. She felt strangely at peace but she missed the little trout motion of the sunlight.

She curled up inside herself in the dusk which was slowly falling and deepening. A bird twittered outside the window, one long note, followed by shorter ones, then there was a silence as if it were listening. In the distance she heard the clink of a pail but no human voices. The bird twittered again. She was listening to it now as if its message was for her, as if it knew that she was lying in there in the darkness.

The light slowly thickened so that the room began to fill up slowly, like a well. Now she could hardly see the wall at all. All hard-edged objects had become softer. She felt that the curtains had ceased moving. Perhaps someone had shut the window. The dusk closed over her. There was no light to be seen anywhere. She closed her eyes again to get away from the dusk.

When she opened them much later the room had changed. Now there was a soft yellow light. And when she looked towards the window she saw the moon, all yellow, shining by itself in the sky, looking in. It was a full moon, very yellow, very warm. It seemed to have a face and eyes like a human face, delicately shaded here and there on the rim of the yellow, looking like one of the maps Iain had. The wall in front of her was now barred with light from the moon, the yellow of corn and the pallor of whitewash. She had forgotten about the spider's web for she couldn't see it high up there in the corner. The moon seemed to be slowly moving away and she couldn't stop it. It was going off and leaving her. She didn't want this to happen, but she couldn't stop it. It had looked her full in the eyes and was now departing as if it had seen enough.

She closed her eyes again against the dusk and the darkening wall. She turned over on her side towards the window, feeling the band on her head. Slowly, carefully, she put her hand up towards it and touched it. She could tell it was a bandage and made of linen. Suddenly she was frightened. What was it for? Why was she in this strange house? Whose bed was this? She opened her mouth and screamed. She thought someone would come running but no one came. Perhaps her voice couldn't be heard. She screamed again, listening restlessly. No one came this time either. She was about to scream again when a great weariness streamed over her. Her eyes shut and she fell asleep. The room filled completely with darkness.

A woman came to the door and listened, then went away again. The woman looked happier than she had done for a long time. There was a stranger – well, not really a stranger – in the house. She hushed the children and made up a bed for them in the kitchen. It had become a game, this putting her fingers to her mouth, and they were liking it. They would now put their fingers to their own mouths if they seemed to be making a noise.

THIRTEEN

She heard a dog barking as if it were chasing a cat or something. There was a flurry of wings as of birds rising and then a squawking. The tart smell of burning tar drifted in through the window. The wall was now buttered with sunlight. A chair sat against the wall. It was a tall straight chair with four slats.

She took her hands out from under the bedclothes and pushed away the blanket on the top, which was creamy with black stripes down the side. She raised her hands, exploring, and they touched the bedboard behind her. She knocked lightly on the bedboard with her knuckles. Beside the bed was another chair. She could feel new energy surging through her. She looked in the direction of the window. In a high blue sky a bird was wheeling, light flashing from its wings. Outside, she heard children shouting and again the squawking of hens and a dog barking.

The door opened and there was Mrs Macleod, smiling at her.

'Would you like some soup?' she was saying.

She looked brisker and more alert than she had ever seen her. The black hair was tied neatly in a bun and looked smoother than she remembered seeing it. Mrs Scott realised she was hungry. 'Yes, thank you,' she said.

Mrs Macleod smiled again and went out. Mrs Scott leaned back on the pillow, completely relaxed, listening vaguely to the sounds which came into the room from outside. Someone seemed to be hammering, perhaps trying to break a stone. But she just lay back there, letting the sounds drift over her. She felt entirely rested. She kept her eyes on the door. After a while Mrs Macleod came in, carrying a tray with bowl of soup on it. She laid it down on the chair and said: 'Can you

sit up?' She helped her to sit up and sat beside her while she
drank the soup which was full of vegetables, carrots,
turnips, onions. She dipped the scone into it, relishing the
freshness and the wetness together. She didn't take long to
finish it, without a word being said. Mrs Macleod wiped her
mouth for her with a cloth, then went out with the tray. She
herself leaned back on the pillows. A child of about six
looked in the door, its fingers in its mouth, but was hauled
unceremoniously into the next room. She was going to say
that she didn't want the child taken away but she didn't say
anything. She didn't have the right.

So this was where she was, Mrs Macleod's house. But she
didn't want to think about why she was here. She felt it was
dangerous to think too much at this time, though various
shadows were edging at her mind. She veered away from
them.

After another while Mrs Macleod returned with a plate of
meat and potatoes.

'You'll be feeling better now,' she said, sitting on the
chair while Mrs Scott ate. She was ravenously hungry. She
couldn't remember when meat and potatoes had tasted so
sweet. The meat was flank, well salted, with the red
sandwiched between the white, and the potatoes were fat
and floury as if they were bursting to be eaten, laughing at
her. The meat melted in her mouth. Soon she was finished.
Mrs Macleod got up and said: 'I'll get you a cup of tea.' So
far she had made no mention of why Mrs Scott was here.
She suddenly thought: Perhaps they put me out of my
house and I can't remember. Perhaps that's why I am here.
But she couldn't remember having been put out of her
house. Nevertheless a hook was fishing at the corners of her
mind but she slid past trying not to see it, trying not to let it
sink itself in her head as she cruised along. How much
better Mrs Macleod looked. Why, she was smiling and
happy as if she had done some wonderful deed which had
changed her. Mrs Macleod came in with the cup. She was
carrying one for herself as well. She sat down on the chair.
She allowed Mrs Scott to drink some tea, then said:

'You'll be wondering why you're here?'

Mrs Scott didn't say anything.

'Well, it was like this. Three days ago you went to see the
minister. You were talking to me and then you went off
across the moor. I was thinking you looked poorly. So I said
to myself after I didn't see you coming back: "I wonder if
anything happened to Mrs Scott?" But I put it out of my
head. I had a lot to do, with Donald away that day.'

Mrs Scott's face clouded. What was this about three days?

'Anyway, I was making some butter when Norman came
in – he's twelve you know – he and another boy were playing
down by the river and he came in at full speed and was
shouting: "Mrs Scott's fallen into the scream." That's what
he said, he was so mixed up: "Mrs Scott's fallen into the
scream." Well, I ran over for Big Betty and she got her
husband and then we met Mr Macmillan so we got you out of
there. You couldn't say a word. We brought you here as it
was the nearest house. And here you are. We had the doctor
and he just said to let you rest. Have you finished your tea?
I'll take it then. I thought I should tell you because you
would be worrying if I didn't.' She continued: 'The minister
was . . .'

'No!'

Mrs Macleod looked at her in surprise.

'Well, he came the day after, you see. He came to the gate
and my man went out to him. You have to understand that
you talked a lot when you were in bed, to yourself, you
understand, and we knew what had happened. So the minister came and he was standing there at the gate wearing that
black hat of his and carrying a walking-stick. My man
Donald stood on this side of the gate and he kept it locked.
He didn't say a word. I was looking out the window, you see,
behind the curtain. Donald told me to stay inside and not to
say anything. He was very angry and I didn't want to say
anything against him. When he goes very white I know he's
angry, though I must say that it's not often. Well, Mr
Macmillan too had told him you were at the minister's, and
he had seen you walking off and he said you looked very sick
but he didn't want to say anything at the time because he
thought it might be something private. Anyway, we all put
two and two together from what you had said now and again,
and Big Betty told us that she thought you had gone to see

the minister about the house. So that was how it was when the minister came to the gate and he was dressed very smart with his hat and his walking-stick and he was wearing gloves.

"'I should like to see Mrs Scott," I heard him say, for I was looking through the window behind the curtains, you understand, and the window was open. Well, my man didn't say anything. He just put his hand on the gate. He looked at the minister, and didn't say a word. The minister raised his voice. It was like a squeak. "I demand to see Mrs Scott," he said. "She is one of my parishioners. If you don't let me in I'll report you." Still Donald didn't say anything. The minister came up to the gate as if he was going to come in anyway. Then I heard Donald speaking. He was quite quiet but his voice carried: "Though you're a man of the cloth," he said, "whatever cloth it is," (that's what he said, "Whatever cloth it is"), "if you try to come into my house I'll do you bodily harm." That's what he said, "bodily harm". I didn't know what to say. I nearly went out to stop him saying things like that to the minister. You'll know that he doesn't go to church. Everyone knows that and they cast it up to me often enough, though they don't say it so often now. And to the children. I mean other people's children have cast it up to my children, and often give them a black eye over it. Anyway, that's what he said to the minister.

'I was very nervous myself. I'm not very strong, you see, but Donald's strong. The people here don't know how strong he is. What he puts in his head, he puts in his feet, as the saying goes. Well, the minister looked at him for a long time and then he turned on his heel. He didn't say a word, and off he went swinging his stick. Donald came back into the house. He was laughing like a boy. "That's the end of him," he said, and he was in a good mood all the rest of the day. "That did me good," he said "I've wanted to do that for a long time." And then he forgot all about it.'

The room seemed to be spinning about Mrs Scott again. She lay back on the bed and the ceiling seemed to rush at her, dizzying her. But she clung to the one idea. If you faint now, Mrs Macleod will be blamed for it. She shouldn't have told me all this but if I faint now she will be blamed. There seemed to be two Mrs Scotts, the one who was speaking in her mind and the one to whom she was speaking. Over and over the one Mrs Scott repeated: 'If you faint now, Mrs Macleod will be blamed for it.' She hung on like a boat in a driving sea, going up and down, up and down, up and down. She pressed her legs against the bedboard and drew a deep breath. The sea steadied. She swam out of it to find Mrs Macleod leaning over her very white.

'I'm all right,' she said. 'Mrs Macleod, I'm all right.'

Mrs Macleod heaved a deep sigh. 'Thank God,' she said. 'Thank God. If you had fainted and all because of my blethering I would never have heard the end of it. Are you sure you're all right?'

'Yes, yes, thank you. I'm right enough. Thank you for the food.' She lay back again. 'I think I'll just sleep for a little while. I'm sorry to be such a bother.'

'You're no bother at all,' said Mrs Macleod, looking at her doubtfully with the cups in her hands. 'Are you sure you're all right?'

'Are you sure you're all right?' she'd say to her mother and her mother would look back at her saying: 'Yes, I'm sure I'm all right.'

Mrs Macleod smiled at her, patted her hand and then was gone. She closed her eyes and slept.

FOURTEEN

The following day she decided to get up. Not that it wouldn't have been easy for her to stay in bed, for she was very comfortable, more comfortable than she had been for a long time. But, at the same time, some instinct was warning her that she must not become too soft or relax too much. It had been a long time since she had been served with food in bed and it was both too late and too early to begin.

In the afternoon she determinedly got out of bed and stood weakly on the floor. She found all her clothes, as she suspected, in the trunk in one corner of the room and her shoes under the bed. There was no mirror so she could not tell what she looked like. But she felt very scraggy and thinner than she had been. Her face had been washed that morning in a blue basin which Mrs Macleod had brought in, and her hair had been combed. Then, after dressing, she straightened her back, assumed a smile, opened the door and went into the kitchen.

At first they didn't see her. Three people were kneeling on the floor playing with toy soldiers. One of them was Donald Macleod, the other two were children: Norman, whom Mrs Macleod had already mentioned by name, and the little girl whose name she did not know. They all seemed to be taking part in some kind of game which made them oblivious to her presence.

'I've got you this time,' shouted Donald triumphantly. 'Your men are caught in a crossfire.'

The little girl stared up at Norman to see what he would do, then bounced excitedly up and down on the floor.

'What are you going to do now?' said Donald, gazing hard at the boy, who was studying the toy soldiers very intently.

'My soldiers are Highlanders,' he said. 'They're not afraid of your crossfire.'

'Huh. All soldiers are afraid of crossfire,' said his father.

'All right then,' said the boy. 'They're going on anyway. You can't kill all of them.'

Donald looked sadly at the boy. 'I was afraid you'd say that. That was what Wellington said at Waterloo. He was talking about Highland soldiers too. Why do Highlanders always get themselves into such hopeless positions?'

'It's not hopeless, father, it's not hopeless. You can't kill all of them.'

'Can I not? See if I don't.'

The little girl was looking from one to the other, serious and excited. She poked her hand forward tentatively to touch one of the soldiers.

'Leave them alone, Marjory,' said the boy quickly. 'They're mine.'

Donald looked at him. 'What did you say, Norman?'

'They're mine, that's what I said.'

'No, Norman, they're not yours. They're for the two of you. I brought them from Edinburgh for the two of you.'

'She doesn't. . . .'

'Norman, they're for the two of you. Anyway, I shouldn't have brought them. They're putting me off my work. I've got some writing to do. Go outside and play. And put them away first. No, not you. Marjory will put them away.'

Marjory made a grab for them and started putting them in their box while Norman stared glumly at the floor.

'Mind you, Norman, there are no woman soldiers. And that's something. It's the women who tidy things up, isn't it?'

'Yes, that's right, father. Girls do that, don't they?'

'Outside, the two of you.' He got up, and as he did so saw Mrs Scott. 'Oh. Should you not be in bed, Mrs Scott?'

Norman was staring at her and so was the little girl, caught in the process of putting the tin soldiers back in the box.

'Can I see them?' she asked Marjory, who looked at her father. When he nodded she came over with them and showed them to Mrs Scott.

'They're very pretty,' said Mrs Scott, picking one of them up and returning it to the box as if dissatisfied. Then she picked another one up and, looking at it, said:

'That's a Highlander, isn't it?'

'Answer Mrs Scott, Norman.'

'Yes, it's a Highlander, Mrs Scott.'

'Yes, my husband used to have a uniform like that. It's very pretty.'

'Now run along, you two,' said their father briskly. 'And say Good day to Mrs Scott.'

Marjory put the box in a drawer in the dresser and then they ran out.

'I'm sorry my wife is out,' said Donald Macleod. 'Are you sure you're all right?'

'Yes, I'm all right.'

'Please sit down.' Donald Macleod seemed rather ill at ease. She sat down. 'The older children are all away from home,' he said at last. Her eyes strayed to the table, covered with papers.

'Sometimes when I'm slack I can manage to do some writing,' he said.

She hadn't realised how sturdy he was. His head was perfectly bald with his hair greying a little round the sides. His eyes were blue and bulbous, and his nose prominent. As he arranged the papers she saw him glance up quickly at her, revealing sharp quick intelligent eyes. He lowered them quickly again.

'I've just come back from Edinburgh, you see, and I brought them that present. You should see Edinburgh, Mrs Scott. The people. You've never seen so many people. I shouldn't like to stay there, though I go there in connection with my work. You feel as if you're closed in. And then there are the lights at night. When you look at the reflections in the people's faces you think they have the plague. I can never get used to the place, the speed at which everything goes.'

He had the papers arranged now in a neat pile.

'Thank you, Mr Macleod, for having me in your house,' she said.

He laughed and then was serious again.

'What would you have done yourself, Mrs Scott? We have to look after each other.' Again she felt these startlingly quick eyes on her and felt that there was a hidden meaning in the words. He continued:

'There was something I meant to say, Mrs Scott. When I was coming home I heard stories that they intend to have us put out of our houses sooner than we think. I saw a good many flocks of sheep. You've never seen so many sheep before. The land is white with them south of us. They'll go through with it. Oh, they'll go through with it all right, Patrick Sellar and the rest of them. You see, Mrs Scott,' he went on, weighing his words carefully, 'to them we're not people. That's what we've got to understand. They don't think of us as people. When I go through to Edinburgh I learn it. Whenever they hear my Highland tongue they half-smile as if I were a fool and they could cheat me as a matter of course. It is this I hate above all.' His face and neck reddened with anger. But then he smiled again: 'When did you hear from Iain?'

'It's months now, Mr Macleod,' she said.

She was trying to take it all in. This was the first time she had spoken to Donald Macleod for years. She didn't know him well. True, he went about the countryside building houses and not everybody could do this. But, after all, it wasn't only in this village that he built them. That was one of the reasons why she didn't know him very well, because he was so often away.

'You know,' he said, 'you were quite right about Iain. Elizabeth wouldn't have done for him. O, true enough, she's very pretty but she wouldn't have done for him just the same,' he said, shaking his head. 'Iain has high standards. He's a bit adventurous. Who isn't at that age? But, no, she wouldn't have done for him. She's seen too much of Glasgow. Like the rest of them, she's only interested in clothes and money and who'll give them to her. If she's lucky she may end up marrying a fat merchant who'll spend all the week cheating everybody and his Sunday praying.'

She thought this speech most peculiar. Though she herself didn't care much for her sister she wouldn't have spoken as freely as this about her to her neighbours, nor would she have run her down like this.

'You'll be wanting to go back to your own house, and I don't blame you,' said Mr Macleod again.

'I saw the elder and the minister,' she said, 'and they wouldn't help me.'

'Do you see these papers?' he said seriously. 'These papers on the table? I'm not a very educated man, Mrs Scott. I wish I had more education. I left school when I was fourteen like the rest of them. But my father had this business and I went into it. Now my father was a great Bible reader and I would never dare argue with him. One day he fell off the roof of a house he was building, because of the rain. He was well over sixty at the time but you couldn't get him to stop working. As he lay there on the ground I knew he was dying, and I knelt beside him. I don't know how it was but as he lay there I thought to myself: There's my father now, he was a great Bible reader, he always went to church, he was a good living man, and there he is on the ground with the blood pouring out of his mouth, all because he slid off the roof because it was raining. I could do nothing about it. So that's what he came to, I thought. But I shouldn't be saying this, Mrs Scott. Please forgive me. What I set out to say was – I mean at the beginning – I have seen and heard of our people being treated like animals and it angers me. So I began to write little articles for little magazines here and there, and then the newspapers. You won't have seen them. Very few have. And I learnt to write as I was going along, because I was angry, you see. I don't do it for my own amusement. I do it to tell the truth of what is happening to us. But I've said enough. You'll think I'm praising myself. That's what people will say. And who am I anyway? I'm just a stone mason and not a very educated one.'

'Did the man on the white horse come and see you too?' asked Mrs Scott.

'Patrick Sellar, you mean? I'm one of his marked ones. Yes, he came to see me. And I told him to leave. But he'll come back. He'll come back all right. I want to tell you a story, Mrs Scott, and after that you can go to your bed. I have a brother and he lives in a village not far from here. Cruachan, you'll have heard of it? Now, my brother is like me in some ways and he's like my father in others. He's very religious for one thing, like my father, but he's stubborn like me. Well, about three years ago when the rumours first started that they were going to put the land under sheep, you remember there was an outbreak of sickness because of the poor harvest. And the Duchess sent her medicines. You'll remember that? Well, when they came with the medicines, the agent she sent – it wasn't Patrick Sellar, he hadn't come then – my brother you see is a very stubborn man, said to this agent:

'"I hear you're going to put us out and put the land under sheep?"

'"Where did you hear that?" said the agent.

'"Never you mind,' said my brother. "I hear it anyway. Is it the truth?"

'The agent hummed and hawed but at the end he was forced to admit that there was something in it. My brother is a tall strong man and when he gets his teeth into something he won't let go. He said:

'"Well, if you came here to keep us healthy so that you can put us out at the end, you can keep your medicines."

'And that's what the agent did.

'Only my brother's child died. She was three years old. And his wife has never forgiven him for it. So you see, Mrs Scott, what I think of Patrick Sellar and his kind.' His voice changed again and he said:

'And now you must go back to bed, and I must get on with my writing. I'll end up an exile yet but I'll tell the truth before I go.'

As she made her way to the door he said: 'Mrs Scott, you'll find my father's Bible in the drawer if you need it.'

FIFTEEN

The following day, sitting outside on a chair in the sun, she wrote a letter to her son. She spent a long time over this letter because it wasn't like the previous letters she had written and because she had to be careful what she said. She wrote in a round childish hand, much as she would have written years ago in school when that Mary Macdonald, long dead, used to swoop on them like a hawk.

'My dear beloved son,' she wrote. 'It is a long time since I didn't get a letter from you. I hope you are well. Be sure to look after yourself, for they say that Canada is very cold.

'I am well myself and you don't need to worry. You will remember Sheila's girl. She brings the water to me every day but the well has been dried up now for a long time and she goes all the way to the spring. I am hoping that I will have the peats home soon. I get eggs every day from the hen. Big Betty comes in every day to ask me if I need anything so you don't need to worry. Death has taken away Domhnull Donn. He was seventy-seven years old and only his wife is left in the house now. There was a lot of people at his funeral.

'I am going to send you a jersey that I made for you but I don't know how to send it.

'I was thinking of sending you crowdie but they say that it would go bad before it got to you.

'I have to tell you that a man. . .'
She stopped, and on further consideration stroked through the last words and began again.

'I have to tell you that I was speaking to Donald Macleod and that he has a good word for you. He was telling me to remember him to you.

'I am closing now with all my love to you, my beloved son.

'Your loving mother, and write soon.'

She read the letter carefully a few times. It was not exactly the kind of letter she usually wrote. She had thought of telling him about the man on the white horse but decided against it. He had enough to worry about. As she was folding the letter up, Donald Macleod came round the corner of the house in his shirt sleeves and carrying a scythe. He said:

'How are you feeling today?'

He was going to continue past her on his way to the shimmering cornfield when something in her attitude stopped him.

'I see you have been writing,' he said.

'Yes,' she said, 'to Iain.'

'Of course.'

'Mr Macleod,' she said at last. 'I wish you would read the letter.'

'But . . .' He stopped. 'Yes, if you like. If you are sure you want that. But I'm sure you can write a better letter than me. I'm not a good letter writer.'

He took the letter and read it rapidly.

'I see you haven't mentioned anything about Patrick Sellar,' he said. 'I think you're wise. You won't want to worry him.'

But he was puzzled by something else as well and he couldn't discover what it was. It hovered like an angry wasp just off the edge of his mind. There was something missing in the letter and he couldn't think what it was, yet she obviously expected him to understand and he knew that it was important to her, this old woman dressed in black sitting in the chair outside his house on a bright summer's day. And he knew it was because of this that she had shown him the letter.

Distracted by the heady scent of the flowers, he cast about in his mind. True, the letter was very bare. There was hardly any news but it was not to be expected that there would be much, for nothing of importance ever happened in the village, until recently and she had decided against writing of that. But that wasn't it: there was something that ought to have been in the letter and wasn't. He brooded. It was as if she was giving him a message but at the same time didn't wish to tell him directly, as if she was relying on his intelligence to work it all out for himself. He tried to think of the letters his father and mother used to write. Strange thing about her, she wasn't as he had imagined she would be. There had been her poor husband whom she had driven off across the seas. And then there had been the way she had brought up that son of hers, always interfering. Really, people like that could be so stupid and could do such irretrievable damage. Did they not see how they appeared to others with their damned destructive pride, destroying both others and themselves? Their self-righteousness, their religious. . . He stopped. So that was it!

He read the letter again very carefully. So that was it indeed! Not a word about God in it from beginning to end, not a word about ministers. Wasn't there something wrong with that ending? Shouldn't it have read 'And may God bless you, my beloved son.' No, nothing at all about God or religion. He put down his scythe carefully and handed the letter back to her. Then he spoke very carefully at first, then more passionately.

'You know, Mrs Scott, living in a small village can be very difficult. And yet whenever I go to Edinburgh I want back to this village. You wouldn't think that, would you? For people talk. They talk all the time. You'd think that was all they had to do. What was it like, those years when you looked after your mother?'

For a moment she stared at him with hatred in her eyes. Then, her fingers clutching the chair and emptying themselves of it, she began to tell. He listened with horror, with great pity. What she told him was outside his experience, but he could understand it. That sacrifice, which he considered absurd, was recognisable. He forgot about the scythe and the corn which he was supposed to be reaping, and was inside that house with that woman, dead to hope. She told him of her mother's attempt to kill herself (why had he sided quite so unthinkingly with the husband before?), about her son Iain, and his going off to Canada. She told him of the emptiness to which she had returned night after night. She told him of the long struggle to bring Iain up, and of the nights she had stayed awake, brooding, and wondering from where the next bit of bread was to come. And as he listened, the scythe forgotten in his hand, it was as if she was relating a history that had always been and might always be, like a sea rising and falling for ever. But, no, he said firmly to himself, it will not always be, this waste, this terrible waste.

A wasp settled on his hand. He hit it venomously, watching the dead body fall to the ground where it struggled for a while with all the poisonous energy of its being, all black and gold, before becoming still after a final quiver. He was thinking that he should have known of all this before. His protest against Sellar, he now thought, might perhaps have been from the mind. No, not all of it but some of it had been. Perhaps some of it had even been vanity. Had he really wanted to get his name in the papers? Was that all it was? No, not all of it, for he remembered his brother's child and, more particularly, his brother, that stern man in love with the truth who was now being crucified by his own wife. But some of what he had written had been purely intellectual, like his chapter, now almost finished, based on that Colonel's book about the Black Watch and showing how well behaved and moral Highland troops had always been. Perhaps he shouldn't be using intellectual arguments at all. Perhaps he should be relying on the pure venom of anger.

But as he stood there listening – no, by now he was kneeling, as if like a child at the breast of a mother who would tell him everything in the form of a story he would never forget – he knew that his hatred was not simply for those who were bent on destroying the Highlands, not simply for the Patrick Sellars, but for the Patrick Sellars in the Highlanders, those interior Patrick Sellars with the faces of old Highlanders who evicted emotions and burnt down love. These people needed a voice to speak for them. Could he be that voice, torn between the world into which they were born and hating the world Patrick Sellar would make for them, his hatred and contempt? Absentmindedly, he stroked the blade of the scythe which he had sharpened to its finest edge, and without thinking found he had a spot of blood on his hand. He turned the scythe so that it was facing away from him and licked the blood with his lips. Then he brought the scythe back to where it had been before.

Listening, he had been transported into a world of such pure horror that his head ached at it. Why had she not told anyone about this before? He looked at the face which was half-turned away from the bright light, the sunshine falling on the old lines which were like a net, and thought of all the pain, and all the dead, and all the sorrow of those who had lived in this world. When she had finished he said:

'You should have told someone of this before.'

She looked at him, her hands crossed in her lap and said simply:

'Who could I have told?'

He found the letter still clutched firmly in his hand, and all sweaty. He handed it to her. What could he tell her? How could he tell her of the destruction which was coming to the Highlands? How could he tell her of that dazzling light of violence which was going to shine soon like a new sword? How could he tell her of a Duke who cared only for money and for his own pleasures, his own paintings? Of a Duchess who during her holidays did beautiful water colours of a Sutherland which would soon be no more? She couldn't understand all this for she hadn't been taught to think on general lines. All she could understand was what was personal. And he knew too that being human she would hate him for this, that in her moment of weakness she had been tricked, as she would consider it, into telling the story of her life. The human heart and the human mind, how infinitely complicated they were! How could one bring them under order? Even Patrick Sellar wouldn't be able to do that. What could he say to her? The space between them, how infinitely large it was, he kneeling and she seated on the chair.

With great patience he sought for something to say, but couldn't find anything at all which would bring him closer to her. So there they were in the humming day, both looking at the ground as if they were effigies, while the summer flowed around them in interpenetrating colour and scent. Finally, he got up and said: 'Thank you for showing me the letter.' He hadn't found the spell which would release them, the word that he could say and she could understand. And this tormented him. Obscurely he felt that it was important to him to find the word and to be able to say it, so that he would be united with her and what she was. Perhaps only the poets would be able to find that word. Or perhaps it didn't exist. But it must exist. Somewhere it lay concealed under lies and differences, like the soot in a black house which could be used to fertilise the land. Somewhere, if he could tear the beams apart, the dry old beams, he would find it and build a new kind of house. For after all, he was a mason. He would find it if he was worthy.

He thought of the day Patrick Sellar had come to his house. This was the enemy, this little man, servant of those who were greater than he.

'We know about you,' Sellar had said. 'We know about your writings. But there's nothing you can do anyway.'

'I can tell the truth.'

'The truth!' Sellar had laughed. 'The truth? What's that? Don't you know that the day has come when the truth is what we care to make it? Surely a man like you who has the reputation of being an atheist ought to know that.'

It was as if for a moment, by a strange wayward luxury, Sellar had almost condescended to argue with someone from the other side whom he recognised to be reasonably intelligent, as if, knowing he would win anyway, he could afford the pleasure of debate.

'No, Macleod, you can't oppose the movement of the age, and that movement is against your old-world survival. Do you know, some day one of you will come to me, having returned from Canada with a map in your hand and a Balmoral on your head, and you'll thank me for having put you in the way of making a fortune? Why, we might even have a glass of whisky together and talk of old times.'

'What about those who won't come back and have lost their maps?'

'My dear Macleod, the progress of civilisation demands sacrifice. Where would the world be if there was no one willing to move into the future? Can you not understand that?'

'Is it moving into the future to send these people into hovels by a sea which is strange to them and to a fishing to which they have never been used?'

'They will grow used to it. The human mind is infinitely adaptable.'

'And what of yourself? Do you wish to emigrate or to live in a hovel?'

'Me? The question doesn't arise for me. You see, Macleod, I'm a lawyer by training. I don't come from the Highlands. I can see your lives, I may say, dispassionately. I state a case and I am very lucky in that I am on the side of the question in which I believe; and, even better than that, one whose answer is inevitable.'

'If it is as inevitable as you say, why do you have to use force? Why can't you wait?'

'There isn't time.'

As he looked at Sellar as they talked together, it seemed as if this confrontation had been going on for ever and would go on for ever, in a time which was palpable as weather itself.

'So you are a happy man, Sellar. On the side of history and making a profit from it?'

Something flickered for a moment in Sellar's eyes, as if it were an insect about to sting.

'Who can say what happiness is, and whether one is ever happy? But there's one thing sure, Macleod, if you don't put a stop to your writings, you won't be very happy.'

He himself had almost been caught for a moment in the net of an academic discussion about happiness which he would have enjoyed. Instead of pursuing metaphysics, he said:

'What can you do about it?'

'Oh, there are many things. Our methods need not be public, but we have them. I can tell you something. No, better still, I'll put it in the form of a question. Whose side do you think the law will be on?'

'Oh, I'm sure the law we have will be on your side.'

'Yes, Macleod, that's the beautiful thing about the law. It's not interested in emotion, as law. And, anyway, are you implying that there is some other law?'

The question was darted out quickly as if Macleod were a witness he was trying to trap into a damaging admission, as if he were saying:

'Well, is it the law of God you're thinking of?'

'Oh, yes, Mr Sellar. There is another kind of law.'

'And which is that?' he asked, turning at the door.

'Perhaps you don't know about it. Have you ever read any poetry? We in the Highlands are very fond of poetry.'

'Poetry?' He was uncomprehending.

'Well, I'll tell you. There are some poets, we call them bards, who have written songs about you. Did you know that? Shall I quote a bit? "Patrick Sellar, I see you roasted in Hell like a herring and the oil running over your head." That, of course, is only part of it. You see, Mr Sellar, you will become a legend. You have become a legend. Are you flattered? Is that perhaps what you wanted? You talk about the future. Yes, true enough, you too will have a future. Children will sing about you in the streets in different countries, countries you will never visit. They may even recite poems about you in the schools. Yes, your name will be on people's lips.'

'Who reads these Gaelic poems anyway?'

'Who, indeed? Nevertheless, they exist. And, who knows, perhaps some day it will be fashionable to read them. The descendants of the class who employ you may take them up out of idleness. You never know what idle people will do. You see, that is a law you didn't know about. It is also a law of the future.'

Patrick Sellar had looked at him for a long time, as if trying to imprint his image on his memory, and then without another word had walked out of the house. Since then he had not seen him. But he would be back, there was no doubt of that. Oh, there was no doubt of that. And he himself might very well end up in Canada, as Sellar had said, in bitterness writing articles that no one would ever read.

'Well,' he said at last, 'I'd better get on with my scything.'

She didn't say anything, almost as if she had forgotten him. As he was going, Big Betty came round the side of the house.

'I came to see the invalid,' she shouted gaily. 'Now you go off and do your scything. She'll be well enough till you come back.'

He went down to the cornfield.

'And how are you, Mrs Scott?' said Big Betty.

'I'm better now. I'll be going home soon.'

'I'm sure you'll be glad of that. Everyone wants to be in his own house. Isn't that right? Well, Mrs Scott,' she boomed. 'They looked after you well here.' And then in a whisper, 'Didn't they?'

'They were very good to me, Betty.'

'Yes, I'm sure of that,' said Betty in a rather disappointed voice. 'When we found you there we didn't know what to say.'

There came to Mrs Scott a thought which left her suddenly almost breathless. Perhaps they had wondered if she had been trying to kill herself! Perhaps that was what they had been thinking all the time. Perhaps that was why Donald Macleod had been questioning her?

Betty continued: 'But we're all very glad that you are all right now. Even my man is asking for you and he doesn't think about anything but himself most of the time.' She whispered again: 'And how is Mrs Macleod keeping?'

'I think she is down in the field. She is quite well.'

'Ah, that husband of hers has a lot to do,' said Betty, raising her voice. 'I have been hearing a lot since you fell ill. The things people say.'

'What about, Betty?'

'Oh, about Mr Macmillan, but you mustn't say a word of this to anyone. Why hadn't he seen that Mrs Scott wasn't herself, they say? But of course I tell them that the poor man was working. How was he to know that you weren't well? Poor fellow, with that sister of his. She's a proper bitch, Mrs Scott, if you'll excuse me.'

'What else do they say?'

'I was meaning to tell you. Did you know that Sheila has a brother who lives farther south than us? And he was put out of his house and has been shifted to one of these houses up by the sea. Well, Mrs Scott, you wouldn't believe the things he told her.'

'What things?'

'Well, I'll tell you, and this is what Sheila told me. He said that when they went up there the houses hadn't been built. They had to build them themselves. Do you know what they were living on? On sea shells, that's what he said. Sea shells. They were starving, Mrs Scott. Mind you, you have to watch what Sheila says to you just the same. But that's what she told me. And another thing, if it hadn't been good weather they would have died. I wonder if there's a chair I can sit on. . .'

'I'm sure if you. . .'

'No, I'll just sit on the stone. Ah, that's better.' She levered herself down with much puffing, her cheeks becoming redder and redder till she had settled herself. 'Well, and they told them they would have boats but there were no boats either. So they had to make a boat. Imagine that, eh? Sheila's brother! And he never was any good with his hands. I mind the day when he couldn't even put the thatch on the house. So they had to build a boat and they went out in it and one of the boys was drowned. Sheila says they never got his body, just one boot. You wouldn't believe it, would you?

'Well, as I was saying, she told me something else. When they were starving some of them used to climb the rocks for eggs of these seabirds. I don't know their names. And do you know, one of them fell and was killed. He slipped on the rock, you see. And that's the place they're going to send us to. Well, there's one thing sure: my man won't like it. He's never climbed anything in his life. He's so scared he won't even climb up the chimney.'

'What else did he say?'

'Isn't that enough, woman? Well, he did say that the cows didn't like the place and tried to run away. The poor beasts! They couldn't get to sleep at night because of the mooing and the lowing. They made tents for themselves, you see. And to think that some of the little boys used to do that in the summer. It's changed days indeed. And how do you think Mrs Macleod will get on?' she whispered. 'Eh? What does himself say about it? I was hearing that he and Patrick Sellar had a quarrel. I don't blame him for that, that little beggar; begging your pardon, Mrs Scott.'

Big Betty heaved herself about the stone in a companionable silence.

'This stone is eating into my buttocks,' she said, 'but I'm resting my feet just the same. They're not what they used to be. And there's something else, Mrs Scott. They are saying that Patrick Sellar will be back soon and this time he will be putting us out. The first time was just a warning. They have to give us notice according to the law. They can't put us out without any warning. They have to give us notice of a week or two. Even the servant girls in Glasgow have to be given their notice so that they can make preparations. Ay, that's the law. It would be terrible if there was no law, wouldn't it, Mrs Scott?' She sighed massively. 'I'm just wondering what we'll do about that big dresser my man's mother had. I'm sure he won't be able to carry it on his back.' This seemed to amuse her and she giggled fatly to herself. 'Anyway, I'm glad to see you looking so well, Mrs Scott.' Then, 'What did the minister say to you?'

When she had told her Big Betty said:

'Ay, his congregation is falling off now, I can tell you, after last Sunday's sermon. He told them that they would have to leave and, do you know, he said they were like the children of Israel – imagine that – saying they would have to put up with tribulations and they would have to cross the desert and they would come to the Promised Land. Anyone would think he was Moses himself, the way he was talking. And then he talked of those amongst us who don't worship God. It was Donald Macleod he was meaning, of course. Everyone else here worships God and goes to church regularly but he said we were great sinners just the same. Mind you, some of them were crying. Imagine Dolly. She was crying and she's been single all her days. What sin did she do? Eh? She's never seen a real man yet, if you'll excuse me, Mrs Scott. And she's always running after the minister though he wouldn't look at the likes of her. It's Mr Brown this and Mr Brown that and Mr Brown can I clean out the church for you.'

She paused, then said: 'They do say that Patrick Sellar has something against Donald Macleod. I wonder what it is.'

'He writes papers about him.'

'What?'

'He writes papers about him. Papers. He had them on the table.'

'Oh, is that what it is? Papers. Do you know what Sheila's other brother says – the lame one – he thinks he knows

everything just because he sits by that dike every day and
speaks to the passers-by. Why even the children are afraid
of him with that stick of his. Well, he says that Patrick
Sellar won't put us out at all, that the Government will stop
him. He says that at the last moment the Government will
take Patrick Sellar down to London and then they'll charge
him. He says that he's read books about it, that if anyone is
doing wrong and putting people out of their houses the
Government will charge him. He says that there's an act and
it says you can't be put out of your house. They were asking
him where he had seen this act and he said he'd seen it in a
book and if he could only find the book he'd tell them about
it. But he says it's a very old act and that's why he can't find
it. They're calling him "The Act" now and he gets redder
and redder in the face and he takes hold of that stick and
you'd think he was going to hit you over the head with it.
His hands are just like glass because he's always out in the
cold weather but they say he's very strong. But I don't like
his moustache. I don't like a moustache on a man. I like a
beard but not a moustache. Your own father had a fine
beard on him, Mrs Scott. Well, I'm glad to see you're
looking so well. I didn't think you were going to get over it
so quickly, but you'll have to look after yourself for a while.'

She got up unsteadily: 'Drat that stone. My backside's all
cut by it.' She leaned closer: 'Ay,' she said. 'Everyone's
saying that we'll have to go quietly, else they'll send the
soldiers after us.'

'The soldiers?'

'Ay, the Highland soldiers. Mind your own man? He
was in one of them regiments as they call them. There's a
place called Fort George where they stay. They're saying
they use the soldiers if people won't move for them. And
they say the soldiers have to do what they're told. Orders,
you understand! When they get their orders they have to do
what they're told. Of course, not all of them are Highlanders. Some of them are foreign. They won't use the ones
who were in the Highlands all the time. They'll use the
other ones who have been foreign. That's what they're
saying anyway.'

'Who was saying that?'

'Sheila's brother told her. They didn't use them on them but he said they used them in another village. You don't know what they'll do. Oh, well, I must be going. Mrs Macleod isn't in, you said?'

'No, she went down to the fields.'

'Ay, she'll be working on the corn, though who knows what will happen to it. Some people aren't cutting it at all. It'll be a handsome soldier who'll take me out of my house, I'm telling you. I've seen the day they would look at me twice. You could put a ring round my waist in those days. You'd think I had nothing to do, the way I go gallivanting around. And do you know another thing I heard? Up there, in the north by the sea, they say the people aren't nearly as friendly. They are all for themselves. You have to knock on the door before you get in. Would you believe that? Ay, if you were sick no one would look after you up there. That's what they say. Well, I must be off this time. And make sure that you look after yourself. Mar sin leat.'

She went off round the house. Mrs Scott could hear her opening and shutting the gate, and then her footsteps on the road. After Big Betty had gone, Mrs Scott still sat there, the letter in her hand, staring unseeingly down towards the cornfield, where she could see the flash of Donald Macleod's scythe. Part of the field was mown, part was not. She could hear the children shouting faintly and a dog barking. And she noticed that there were few people working in the fields, just as Big Betty had said.

Suddenly on an impulse she arose and went into the house. She stood for a moment hesitantly in the doorway of the kitchen, not at first knowing what she wanted to do. Then she walked over to the dresser where the toys had been put away. She opened the top drawer and there was the box. She didn't open it, only glanced at the picture on the outside, two regiments drawn up facing each other, some on horses and some not. She shut that drawer and opened the next one. Immediately she recognised the papers that Donald Macleod had had on the table. She took them out and glanced at them. Among them was a paper with 'Edinburgh Gazette' written on it. She put it down and found a book below it. She opened it but couldn't make anything of it. The author seemed to be some kind of foreigner. There were long words in it which she did not understand but here and there she saw words which she recognised, like 'crofts' and 'Sutherland'. She put it away, thinking that if she had been cleverer she would have been able to follow it, and regretting her lack of education.

Then she turned to the papers written by Donald Macleod himself. She took one of them over to the light and began to read it. It said 'The Highland Clearances' by Donald Macleod. She could understand some of it. He talked of the Highland regiments and how they had made themselves famous all over the world and how the men were coming home to find that their crofts had been burnt to the ground. But she was still dissatisfied. It wasn't what she wanted, though she didn't know what she wanted. She put it down with the other papers, then closed that drawer.

She opened another which was full of clothes, children's clothes, all the time thinking that she wished she could understand more clearly what all these papers were about. Beneath the clothes she found a portrait of an old man with a white moustache and a beard and an angry looking face. It was most likely Donald Macleod's father. She looked at it for a moment and then put it back, glancing at the clock. It was three o'clock. She rummaged about but found nothing else in that drawer.

She opened the bottom one. She found a small packet of letters tied with a rubber band. She held the rubber band and pulled the letters out. Then she looked out of the window but could see no one. Trembling, she opened the first letter which looked yellow with age and had a queer old fashioned handwriting.

Dear Emily (it said)

How I yearned for you when I saw you in church today, with your beautiful new bonnet. I am sure that every eye was on you as mine was, even in this douce city of Edinburgh. How I wish that I, a poor student, were as rich as our merchants and that I could give you silks for your dress and diamonds for your hair. But of one thing I am sure – no one can love you as much as I do. And do not write to me in future that you are but a poor servant girl and I am a student. You might as well say that I am a 'poor' student who is almost neglecting his books because of you – but do not blame yourself for that! It is you also who maintain me when I am weary of the books, the law, its grammar and its barrenness. Oh, if you know how much I long for you! But then I think of my good fortune that you should exist at all and that I should have met you, which is the greatest good fortune of all. I can almost forgive addle-pated Mackay for having been so accidentally clever as to have singled out for lodgings the place in which I should meet you. Shall I see you this Monday night? Please write at once to say that I shall, for otherwise I tell you with hand on heart that I shall throw myself from Arthur's Seat.

Your half-demented
Robert

Hastily she turned to the next letter, dated a month later.

My dear Emily,

I write this at midnight. Listen. The bell has just tolled. Do you not hear it? Of course you can hear it. I fancy that it unites us as it united us last night. Why do I write? I can't tell except that my feelings demand utterance. My sweet one, how could I have known? How could we have known? Shall I always hear that cry of a startled thrush – was it a thrush? And that moon – shall I remember it always? It was I, I who was to blame, if blame there was. Yet how could we have foretold how the blame itself – the sense that there would be blame – was overwhelmed by that other sense. My dear Emily, how in future I must curb myself though the Devil himself were tempting me! How chaste we shall be, though God knows how much I shall long to take you in my arms. The bell has completed its tolling.

From me to you at midnight,

Yours for ever,
Robert

My dear Emily, (dated much later)

I cannot sleep for thinking what you told me. What

Fury is it that drives me to writing, for what will writing
avail? But it is as if when I'm not with you in the flesh I
need to be with you in the spirit, and I had thought the
writing of letters would be sufficiently harmless.

What are we going to do? (I do not wish to worry you
but I am writing this out as if to find an answer to our
troubles.) Not that I regret – even if I felt blame – what
we are to each other. But I foresee the future and know
what will be. You should not trouble yourself so much
about the future. There will always be something to do.
But though large, Edinburgh is really a small town and
soon they will be at our throats. Do not deceive
yourself. The minister who condescends to talk to you
now when he visits your master and mistress will soon
be an enemy. And do not imagine that you will be
allowed to maintain the situation that you have. You
and I will be outcasts. We have to confront this in all its
truth. . .

Slowly spelling out the letters, Mrs Scott in her intense
interest had forgotten herself. Very gently a hand removed
the letter from her hand. Very gently the hand put the letter
back in the band, replaced all the letters in the drawer and
shut it. Very gently Donald Macleod said:

'Well, I must confess that that is a habit of my own, Mrs
Scott. I have a natural curiosity which nothing can abate.
You know, a lot of people have wondered about me. A man
who keeps himself to himself must expect that curiosity.
What do you think of these letters?' he asked, looking at her
keenly.

'I don't know,' she said hesitantly, looking down at the
ground. 'I'm sorry. I didn't. . .'

He laughed. 'You don't think they are family letters?' he
said at last. 'No, no. Mrs Scott, I'm not illegitimate or
anything like that. These letters . . . I'll tell you now how
they came into my possession. One day I wandered through
Edinburgh and I came to this man who was selling books
from a barrow, old books. And I looked through them. You
haven't heard about novels, Mrs Scott?'

No, she hadn't heard about novels.

'Yes, well, they're stories that people write to amuse

themselves. I sometimes read one or two when I have time.'

Naturally she didn't know anything about novels.

'Well, I picked out this particular book carelessly and then when I opened the book I found these letters inside the cover. I don't know whether they are real letters or whether they are part of a book the man who had the novel originally was going to write. You can't tell. Do you think they're real?'

'I don't know,' said Mrs Scott in a confused manner, still ashamed of herself for having been so absorbed in them that she hadn't heard Donald Macleod approaching. 'They were very beautiful,' she said at last.

'Yes, they are in a way,' said Donald Macleod off-handedly. 'Though I must say that the style doesn't appeal to me.'

She didn't know what he meant by style.

'Please forgive me,' she said with a curious dignity. 'I don't know why I did what I did after your hospitality.'

'Don't say anything more about it, Mrs Scott. It just shows that you're interested in human beings, that's all. It's a good thing.'

But she wondered just the same why she did it. Was it because she wanted to find out something shameful about him, some weakness he had been concealing all these years?

'I should like to go home tomorrow, Mr Macleod,' she said at last.

'Yes. Yes, of course. But only if you want to, mind. Only if you're feeling well enough.'

'Mr Macleod?'

'Yes?'

'I'm sorry I can't understand your writings.'

'Oh, these. Who can? Don't worry about that, Mrs Scott. You're not the only one.'

'You're a very strange man.'

'Oh, I'm not so strange. It's just that because I'm playful people don't think I'm serious. They think in the Highlands that only serious people are serious. You know, I should have let the minister see these letters. It would have given him ammunition enough. You must admit that I could have great fun from them. Why, I could even change the names.'

Then, more seriously, 'You know, Mrs Scott, your son and I used to have great talks.'

'I know.'

'I suppose you disapproved of them. But I never spoke to him about religion. I just think there should be more fun about. I nearly said to you just now that Emily was supposed to be my mother, and I could have built up a marvellous story, just for fun. Would you have believed me?'

'I know that your mother's name wasn't Emily.'

'Ay, that would have spoiled it right enough. And you shall go home tomorrow if that is what you want. But don't think we won't miss you. It did my wife good to nurse you. She'll be back in a minute. She likes nursing people, especially old people. I haven't seen her so happy for years. And these letters, now. They're quite beautiful in a way. Aren't they? I suppose there must be a reason why I kept them. I don't know. I like these old things. And there's something very touching about them. Even I can feel that.' He paused, then said: 'It's funny how you can't tell whether they are real or part of a book a man was going to write. They sound real just the same. There are stories like that in the Bible too,' he added with a smile, 'only they took place much longer ago, and not in Edinburgh! I thought at first they were real too, but there was something about the style, something that didn't quite ring true. No, I think someone made them up. I think they're fiction.'

SIXTEEN

Night fell over Spain, over Canada, over the Highland villages, over the sheep and the sheepdogs, over the shepherds, over castle and thatched house, over London, over old and young, over the couple making love in the cornfield, over the old people turned away from each other.

And she dreamt an old woman's dreams. She dreamt of her husband on a white horse putting her out of the house with a gun in his hand. She dreamt of her son writing letters to Elizabeth and hiding them in an old dresser. A man in a black gown was standing at a door and behind him a river was flowing. In the river was a dead sheep with a human face, and she could not tell whose it was. Big Betty was standing on the bridge waving a letter and shouting words which she could not hear. The river became a torrent and huge rocks rose on each side of it. A boy was climbing one of the rocks while a piper played below. The boy turned his smiling face and she saw that it was Iain. As he climbed she looked again at the piper but he had changed. He was now a drunkard capering about and lashing himself with a whip. His face was her husband's face. He was grinning at her and posturing on the cliff, at the top of which a man was preaching a sermon, his gown flowing in the wind. Again she couldn't hear a word he was saying though his mouth opened and shut.

The scene changed. There was a room and in the room a man was writing a book. The book appeared to be a Bible but the man was writing on its pages as if they were blank. He would look up thoughtfully now and again as if thinking and then continue writing. When he was finished he put the Bible away in a big box in which he rummaged. He brought dresses and a ring. A little girl came in and he put the ring on her hand and she danced out again. Then he went into another room where someone was lying on a bed. He took another big book from beside the bed and took it down to the table as before and began to write on the pages as if they were blank leaves. Then he locked it away again. The person on the bed couldn't move and she couldn't make out whether it was a man or a woman.

Mrs Scott sighed and turned restlessly in her bed. She seemed to be speaking but the man, standing at the bedroom door, couldn't hear what she was saying as she lay there in the moonlight, though he could see her lips move. He listened for a long time and heard her sigh again. Everyone was in bed but himself and the lamp was lit in the kitchen. His face looked grimmer than it had done when he was talking to her that afternoon. It was as if he were debating something within himself. After a long time his face changed and became more tranquil, as if he had come closer to an answer though perhaps he had not yet fully perceived it.

Mrs Scott turned restlessly, her dark shape humped, but he didn't go near her. Instead, he went back to the table and began to write in the glow of the lamp. This was the time when he could get most of his writing done. He looked up his book by the Swiss economist and read of what had happened to the Swiss peasants, and of what the author had to say about the Highlands. After a while he pushed the book away impatiently and put down the pen with which he had been taking notes. His brow wrinkled as if he were thinking out not a speculative problem but a personal one to which there was no ready answer. Later, he put his papers away and went to bed.

SEVENTEEN

Mrs Scott did not leave the Macleods till the following afternoon, as she was asked to look after the two children in the morning. It was Donald Macleod who asked her to do this.

'We'll be working in the field,' he said, 'and we'll have to try to get it finished. You never know, the weather might break soon.'

But there was no sign that the weather would break. The day was like the previous ones, perfectly blue, perfectly clear, perfectly balanced. Lines suddenly swam into her mind like a fish rising out of a haze, lines from an author whose name she could not recall, if they had an author:

O mosglamaid gu suilbhir ait
le sunndachd ghasd is eireamaid.

Lines in praise of a summer morning and one's urge to get up and be about in it.

So she found herself alone with the two children. The dishes had all been washed and put away. At first the boy was suspicious and went over to the dresser by the open window, then began to hunt about in the drawers. He took out the toy soldiers, laid them on the floor and stared at them half-heartedly. The girl looked at Mrs Scott. Then she too went over to where the boy was. She poked at the soldiers.

'Do you like going to school?' said Mrs Scott at last to the boy, for want of something to say.

'No.'

There was a silence. Marjory got up from the floor, and stood looking at Mrs Scott.

'You took off your blandage,' she said at last, accusingly.

'Bandage, not blandage,' said Norman, impatiently and crossly.

'No, I don't need it now,' said Mrs Scott.

'I found you in the stream,' said Norman suddenly. 'What were you doing in the stream?'

'I fainted. I fell in.'

'Oh.' He seemed disappointed.

'We get trout there,' he said at last. 'We catch them with our hands. Have you ever caught any trout?'

'No, but my son used to catch them.'

'Does he go to school?'

At this point Marjory began to laugh uproariously.

'A soldier fell,' she said triumphantly. 'He fell.' And sure enough one of the soldiers had fallen on its side.

'No, he's too old,' said Mrs Scott.

'Are you going home today?'

'Yes.'

'Well, I don't like school. They give us sums. I like English Composition, but I don't like sums.'

Marjory had planted herself in front of Mrs Scott and was shouting:

'Tell us a story, Granny Scott. Tell us a story, Granny Scott.'

Her brother turned to her and said in someone else's voice:

'Don't be so impudent, Marjory.' Then he turned away from her. 'I got a worm yesterday, Mrs Scott. It was under a big stone, and I took it along to the river to see if a trout would come after it.'

'And did it?'

'Did what?'

'Did a trout come after it?' It was really so difficult to follow the conversation of children, they seemed to be dancing about all the time.

'No, they said a trout would come after it but it didn't.'

'Who said that?'

'Billy and Dell said, but it didn't.'

'Tell us a story, Granny Scott.'

'Will you keep quiet, Marjory? She's only five, Mrs Scott. Do you always wear black clothes?'

'Yes.'

'My mother sometimes wears black clothes. Will we get a holiday if they put us out of the house?'

'What did you say?'

He looked at her scornfully.

'If they put us out will we get a holiday?'

'I suppose so.'

'Good. I hate Miss Macdonald. She hits the desk with a ruler. And she puts spit on the slate.'

'Spit?'

'She doesn't use the cloth. She puts spit on it.'

Marjory came up close. 'Tell us a story, Mrs Scott.'

A story? What story? She had no stories. She couldn't remember any stories. And yet, long long ago, she knew that there had been stories though she couldn't remember any of them.

'My father always tells her stories,' said Norman contemptuously.

'Sometimes he reads them out of a book.' He obviously didn't expect her to tell a story.

'Yes,' she began, hearing her own voice with some surprise. 'I will tell you a story.' She stopped, and then began: 'Once upon a time there was a man. . .'

'What did he look like?'

'He was small and fat and he . . . yes, he carried a whip in his hand. And he rode a white horse.'

There was no other story that she could think of.

'A white horse? I've never seen a white horse.'

'Yes, he rode a white horse and one day he came to this house.'

'What was the house like, Granny Scott?'

'The house? It was like . . . it was a very old house.'

She added triumphantly, 'It had a chimney.'

'Was the chimney very big?'

'No, it wasn't very big. It wasn't a very big house and the chimney wasn't very big. Well, the little fat man rode on his white horse till he came to this house. Then he got off his horse and tied it up.'

'What did he tie it to?' Norman asked. He hadn't really been listening.

'There was an iron stake in the ground they used to tie the cows to.'

'We've got one of those,' said Norman.

'Yes. So he tied his horse to this iron stake and he went to the door and he . . . he banged on the door with his whip.'

'How could he bang with a whip?' Norman spoke again.

'It had a thing at the top of it, a knob made of gold.'

'Oh, I see.'

'Gold?' said Marjory, round-eyed.

'Yes, it was made of gold, and he banged on the door with it and an old woman. . .'

'I bet she was a witch,' said Marjory, jumping up and down. 'I bet she was a witch. Wasn't she, Granny Scott?'

'No, she . . .' then realising that Marjory was becoming disappointed, she said: 'She didn't know she was a witch.'

Marjory looked at her uncomprehendingly.

'All right then,' Mrs Scott surrendered. 'She was a witch.'

'Anyway, the old woman went to the door to see who was there.'

'Did she have a cat?' Marjory asked. 'Witches always have a cat.'

'Yes, she had a cat. She went to the door, and the man said' (here her voice became stronger) '"Am I speaking to Mrs Mackay?" And she said: "Yes" and he said. . .'

She didn't know what to say next. Marjory looked up at her and said:

'She had put a spell on his horse.'

'Yes, that's right, she had put a spell on his horse. Yes, that's right. "He won't do what I tell him," said the man to her.'

'How could she put a spell on a horse?' said Norman scornfully.

'Ah, you don't believe it but I've seen it. There was an old woman here who used to put a spell on the cows so that they wouldn't give any milk, and there was another one and she used to tell when a person was going to die. She would come into the ceilidh house with her feet and her clothes wet and she would say that she had been carrying that person's coffin across a river. . .'

Marjory had fastened on the essential point.

'She put a spell on his horse?'

'Yes, and he said: "This horse used to go anywhere I asked him and he used to go to all the houses and I would put the people out of the houses but –"'

'Why was he putting the people out of all the houses?'

'He was an . . . officer,' she said lamely.

'You mean official, don't you Mrs Scott?' said Norman looking at her keenly.

'Official? What's official?' said Marjory.

'Mrs Scott means that the Government sent him,' said Norman.

Mrs Scott continued desperately, 'And he said to the witch: "You put a spell on my horse and he didn't want to come to your house. See," and he took her out, and she saw that the white horse was all covered with blood, because he had been whipped so badly. And she went up to the white horse and was going to pat him but the man said: "Leave him alone."'

'I know about the white horse,' said Norman.

Marjory turned on him. 'You keep quiet. You're always spoiling my stories.' Surprisingly, Norman did keep quiet and Mrs Scott felt more and more uncomfortable.

She stumbled on: 'And he was covered with blood. And the man said "I want you to take the spell off my horse, because he won't do what I tell him, or I'll come back with a lot of men and put you out as well." So the witch didn't know what to do. She had put the spell on the white horse but she hadn't covered him with blood. It was the man who had whipped him. And, anyway, the white horse didn't really belong to the man. The white horse didn't like the man. The man had taken the white horse from someone else, and the white horse didn't understand what the man was saying to him.'

'What sort of spell had the witch put on the white horse?'

'The white horse didn't like the witch and he didn't like the man,' she said vaguely. 'The white horse came from a foreign place. He used to belong to the army and he was very happy and then he was taken about to put people out of their houses.'

'And he didn't like it.'

'Perhaps the witch didn't put a spell on him at all,' said Marjory. 'Perhaps the man was just saying that.'

'No, she had put a spell on him,' Mrs Scott insisted. 'And the horse didn't know what to do. Anyway, after the man had told this he got on his horse which was snarling and trying to throw his rider off, and he told her that she would have to take the spell off or he would come back and put her out. But the witch shouted at him, "Your white horse will never come back," and he shouted back, "Yes, he will come back." So she sat down. . .'

'With her cat . . .' said Marjory.

'With her cat, and she thought what she would do.'

'She thought and thought,' said Marjory.

'Yes, she thought and thought. All that day she thought and thought. And the next day, and the next night. For three days and nights she thought and thought but she didn't know what to do. So on the fourth day she got up and she took her broom – no, I'm telling a lie – just when she was going out another witch came to see her. . .'

'Another witch?'

'Yes. And the two of them talked about it and she said: "What am I going to do about the white horse?" And the other witch said, "There's nothing you can do about the white horse." And he. . .'

'You said it was a witch.'

'Yes, and she said: "You can't do anything about the white horse or they'll put a spell on you." So the witch went away and after a while she began to cry because she thought the other witch would help her.'

'Was she a big witch?'

'Yes, she was a big witch. Anyway, she went away and the other witch thought and thought. For seven days and seven nights she thought and thought, and then she said to herself: "I am going up to the castle where the chief of all the witches lives." So she put on her head dress and her black overall. . .'

'Gown.'

'Black gown and she took her broomstick and she went off. And she came to a deep. . .'

'You're doing very well,' said Donald Macleod, coming in smiling. But she knew that she wasn't, and that she couldn't tell a proper story. All the time she had got more and more muddled and she didn't even know how the story was to end.

EIGHTEEN

She was back in her own house again. Donald Macleod had lit the fire before he left her, and she was sitting in her own chair once more. After the turmoil and noise she rested, closing her eyes and listening to the sound made by the fire leaping up the chimney. The brown peat burned quickly and left only a little ash behind it. The black peat burned more brightly with a white radiance.

Around her, the house was absolutely silent except for the sound made by the pendulum of the grandfather clock, which she had rewound. It felt, however, curiously tranquil, as if some pressure had been removed from it. She had looked with a certain amount of surprise at the plates which she had left on the table before she had gone to see the minister. They seemed to belong to a distant world. She had smiled, realising that this had been the longest period she had ever been out of her house, the best part of a week. And so many things had happened to her in just a week – the man on the horse, the journey to see the minister, her fall into the stream, the waking in a strange room, the talks to Donald Macleod, the incident of the letters, and the story of the witch. Tired by them, yet in some way refreshed, she dozed contentedly while the fire crackled in the chimney. She felt better than she had done for years.

Two hours must have passed like this before her first visitor came. This was Sheila who had come to ask her about the ring she had given the Linnet. She had forgotten all about it.

'Yes, I gave her the ring,' said Mrs Scott.

'Oh, that's all right then. But you see she. . .'

'No, she didn't steal it,' said Mrs Scott.

Sheila looked at her in surprise for stating her own

suspicions so bluntly.

'Oh, I don't mean that. It's just that you shouldn't give her any presents for taking the water in to you.'

'It was a ring I used to have myself. It's not worth much.'

'In that case I'll give it back to her. I must admit she said you had given it to her. To tell you the truth, she was crying. She will come tomorrow as usual.'

'Thank you.'

Sheila looked at her curiously and then said:

'It's not easy to bring them up. Sometimes you're too soft and sometimes too hard. But she's a good girl, no matter what anyone says. She has a heart of gold.' She continued: 'But sometimes William doesn't feel well and we get behind with the work and then . . . well, there are others with more money than us and the children are at us to. . .' William was a big fat apparently jovial fellow who had been working on a stone house for at least four years but much of the time he stood in his canvas jersey gazing vaguely down the road, his barrow abandoned beside a partly-unearthed stone. 'And it's even worse now because no one wants to do anything in case we have to go.'

'Is that what's happening?'

'Yes, I'm not looking forward to it after all those years. I just don't know what we're going to do. Imagine all these children by the sea. We'll have to watch them all the time. We won't get anything done. They might pick things up and poison themselves. And there'll be strangers. You won't know who they'll be mixing with. But the better-off ones will be all right,' she said bitterly. 'And the strong ones. Big Betty will be all right. She's as strong as a horse. The likes of us won't be so well off.'

'So they're all going, then?'

'Oh, they are. One thing I hope is that it will be good weather. Think if it was pouring with rain. Everything would be ruined. Not that I have so much, but a few things I have got in Glasgow. But if the rain comes on, then I don't know what will happen. And where's the well to be? I ask them. Are we going to drink salt water? But they don't know anything about it. They're leaving it to the last minute. Except Murray; he'll make a good thing out of it with his

cart. The people who can pay him, they'll get all their goods
up there. Well, as they say there won't come a low tide
without a high tide after it, perhaps it won't be so bad as we
think.' She got up. 'Anyway, thank you for the ring but you
shouldn't be giving her things.'

'Wait a minute,' said Mrs Scott, and on an impulse went
up to the other room, rummaged about in the chest and
found an old globe which her husband had once bought for
Iain. She held it in her hands for a moment, then below it
she saw a pair of green stockings with orange diamonds at
the top which she had once knitted for him. She took them
out quickly and went into the room where Sheila was,
peering at the flowered cups displayed on the dresser. She
turned when she saw Mrs Scott, who said:

'And give these to the boys. They won't be so jealous of
the ring then, and she won't have to hide it.'

'Oh, how beautiful, Mrs Scott! Did you knit them
yourself? But of course you did. I used to envy the way you
dressed Iain with all those lovely woollen suits. I don't know
where you learned to do it.'

'My mother taught me,' said Mrs Scott briefly, adding
after a while: 'She was a good knitter till she fell sick.'

Sheila held the globe in her hands, staring at it without
comprehension.

'And this is very pretty too with all the different colours,'
she said.

'It'll help him with his schooling,' said Mrs Scott.

'Ay, but I'm afraid that Danny isn't very good at his
lessons, not like some who become ministers and school
teachers.' Sheila stared vaguely out of the window, the
globe spinning restlessly in her hands. 'But we can't all be
clever,' she said at last, 'though I'm sure we would all wish
it.'

'No, we can't,' said Mrs Scott, thinking of the minister.

'I often wish I had learned my lessons better,' said Sheila.
'But I didn't have a good head. Many's the time I was
thrashed for it. But a good thrashing doesn't do anyone any
harm. Still, as they say, what comes in at one ear goes out
the other. Anyway, thank you Mrs Scott, for the lovely
stockings and the globe. And be sure to ask if you want

anything done. She's not doing much anyway and it keeps her out of mischief.'

Then she was gone, carrying the globe with her, awkwardly nestled under her arm, looking rather comic in a way.

Her second visitor was Mr Macmillan, who came to ask her how she was. He sat on the seat where Patrick Sellar had sat, his huge red hands protruding from his cuffs and his cap beside him.

'I am sorry I did not come to ask you if you were well,' he said with the embarrassment of one who is not used to visiting people much. At one time he had been a postman but the responsibility had proved too much for him, for he would deliver his letters only to those to whom they were addressed even though this meant, as it often did, going down to the fields to hand them over to them. He wouldn't even give them to members of the addressee's family.

'You don't have to blame yourself, Mr Macmillan,' she said. He didn't seem to have anything to say so she added:

'And how is your sister?'

'She is as well as we can expect, praise be to God.'

'I am glad to hear that.'

'Yes, I don't know what I'll do when we have to leave. She doesn't like being moved from her bed. But God in his mercy will send sustenance in his own time.' There was another long silence while he twisted and untwisted his cap. Then he said:

'Perhaps it is God's will that we have to go. We do not know the day or the hour.'

Suddenly he got up: 'I only came along to find out how you were. I can't leave her for long,' he said confusedly. She didn't know why he had come. Had he heard that some people were saying he was to blame? Even the good have to suffer scandal, she thought.

'You're not to blame,' she said. 'How could you have known?'

The eyes brightened in the reddish weather-beaten face.

'I'm glad to know that you think that. Glad to know. . .' he mumbled. 'Perhaps I think of myself too much. . .'

Then, ducking under the low-lintel, he too was gone, abashed and happy. And she was left alone again, feeling curiously restless as if she were waiting for something to happen, walking about the house touching this object, then that. The restfulness she had felt when she came back first had worn off. She went to the window and looked out as if expecting to see someone else come to the door, though she did not know whom she could be expecting. She was listening for voices but they were voices containing laughter. Whom did she expect to see, walking or dancing up to the door demanding admittance? Yet all she could see was what she always saw, fields, houses, fences, a road with no one on it, ditches empty of water and slowly darkening.

This was the time of night, she realised, when there would be the music of the melodeon. But there was no music tonight. Perhaps there would never be music again. And she realised she was sorry. Perhaps she had loved that music all her days and someone had taken it away from her. So many of the dancers were now at the ends of the earth, or under it, so many occupied with fighting pain, and so many old. Why, even Mr Macmillan had danced there at one time: even his sister had been as gay as the rest. So had Sheila before she got married to the fat lazy man who had probably lain with her, in his more handsome days or nights, in a cornfield in the autumn. And the footballers too, all the young footballers had streamed home across the moor, sweating and high coloured in their big tackety boots, their short trousers and their long. In the ghostly moonlight they had played, shooting a ghostly ball into a ghostly goal mouth, diving and dribbling about in the ebbing light as if under water. Were they still there – presences on the moor and at the end of the road? No, she said firmly, turning away from the window. They are not still there. Nor is there anything in the shadows but shadows. And, bolting the door, there is no one here but me and I'd better send that letter to Iain tomorrow. The Linnet can take it when she's going to the spring for water. And no, she decided. I won't tell him anything about what happened to me. And it's time I was going to bed. I'm getting too old for fairies. And I will have to live the way I am and I do not regret telling Donald Macleod what I told him.

Now someone else knows it too and I won't have to speak of it again. She undressed by the light of the lamp, slowly and deliberately, put out the light and went to bed.

But she prayed just the same, knowing that never again would she go to that church and that her Sundays here were for ever her own. For hadn't the long years of sacrifice taught her anything? Yes, they had taught her to endure more than she thought she could endure. And you couldn't judge God by his servants. As well as this, you could find God in those who weren't his servants. This might not last but for tonight it lasted, and she had learned to get through her life, night after night and day after day. Hadn't Christ himself said: 'Take no thought for the morrow, for the morrow will take care of itself'?

And the light of the lamp was yellow like the lily. . .

And she slept.

NINETEEN

On the following day Patrick Sellar returned. This time he had another man with him. And they were on horseback as before, one on a white horse and one on a black horse. This other man was taller than Patrick Sellar, calmer, thinner, speaking less, watching more, and greater than Patrick Sellar, for when Patrick Sellar spoke to him he spoke to him gently as a servant does to a master. But this other man was watching everything all the time, even Patrick Sellar. Yet he wasn't the Duke for she had seen the Duke. And this other man's eyes seemed to see more deeply yet more calmly than the small hot ones of Patrick Sellar. They were very blue eyes which after a while you came to notice.

This time they knocked on the door. The man with Patrick Sellar had thought of that, she was sure, for she wasn't quite as innocent as she once had been. But she didn't offer them tea though she was sure they would have accepted it while the white horse and the black horse chewed the grass outside in an air which had become slightly thundery. And this time Patrick Sellar carried a big wallet with papers in it, though she was sure he was carrying it for the other man.

'Mrs Scott,' said Patrick Sellar, after he had sat down on the seat. The other man looked round the room, then at her, and sat on the chair. 'This is Mr John Loch.'

'I am pleased to meet you, Mrs Scott.'

And he sounded as if he meant it, looking at her curiously.

'Now, Mrs Scott,' said Patrick Sellar, coming down to business. 'You will remember that I was here before and you will remember what I said to you.'

She didn't answer.

'And you might have taken away a bad opinion of me. But we understand that. It is not easy for an old woman to leave her house.'

Mr Loch seemed to be studying Patrick Sellar, as much as he was studying her, sitting there so quietly, waiting.

'I spoke to Mr Loch about you and he knows all our conversation.'

He looked at Mr Loch who made no sign.

'But further. . .'

'Circumstances,' said Mr Loch. He had a habit of not appearing to be listening, and screwing up one of his eyes, looking around him all the time.

'Further circumstances have come to our attention which put your case in a new light. I think it is fair to say that,' went on Patrick Sellar, with a slight questioning air as if he were holding a secret dialogue with his master, who spoke suddenly.

'Yes, Mrs Scott. Certain new circumstances have arisen which made us have a second look at your case.' He signed almost imperceptibly to Patrick Sellar to continue.

'You see, Mrs Scott, we have heard from your minister, a very fine man – oh, nothing against you Mrs Scott, in fact he gave the highest account of you – we have heard of a certain incident which occurred recently.'

'You see, Mrs Scott,' said the other man. 'The minister tells us that you are acquainted with a person known as Donald Macleod, a confessed atheist. Now, we know that under normal and usual circumstances this acquaintanceship would not be voluntary – on your part.'

'Mr Loch means of your own free will.'

'Thank you, Mr Sellar. We cannot believe – your minister and I and Mr Sellar – we cannot believe that a woman such as you, brought up on Christian principles, would of your own free will associate with such a man, and therefore we believe – and Mr Sellar is quite willing to blame himself for this. That is, leaving you in a state of loneliness which would drive you to seek the help of such a man, if seek his help you did and he did not impose it on you – in fact we believe that Mr Macleod did at one point prevent you from seeing your minister. Now Mrs Scott, you don't need to answer just yet.'

'In your own interests, Mrs Scott, you should listen to the proposal which Mr Loch will put to you.'

'Mrs Scott, I'm afraid I will have to make a long speech and you will have to be patient with me. I have the honour of advising the Duke of Sutherland, who is also your chief. Some years ago the Duke, whom I have the honour of serving, decided that in the interests of humanity these villages, in one of which you live, should be eliminated and that their population should be moved to the north to the coast, there to subsist on fishing from which in the course of time a thriving industry should emerge. To this end he considered long and carefully, moved thereto by the number of instances of famine which had been reported to him in recent years and the evident difficulty under which these people were labouring in making their livelihood here. Now, as a woman of intelligence, you will see that in this the Duke was exercising humanity and generosity. Not that he grudged the money and resources with which to relieve such famines but that he believed it would be in the interest of the people to remove themselves, for in this new region they would find better houses, an abundance of fish and the opportunity to make a better life for themselves. You understand all this? Good.

'I was given the signal honour of being put in charge of the proceedings and I can say, Mrs Scott, that I haven't regretted such an opportunity. You will imagine, therefore, how astounded I was when in certain newspapers and journals I read remarks by a certain Donald Macleod in which, by building a fabric of lies, he was seeking to destroy all that I was doing. Mr Sellar, will you please read portions of what this Donald Macleod has written so that Mrs Scott will understand more clearly what we have come to say?'

'Certainly, Mr Loch. Mrs Scott, I pick these passages, as you will see at random. Please listen carefully. This is what Mr Macleod had the temerity to write: "It is clear, therefore, that not content with sending our soldiers to die on the field of battle for what they do not understand, these men – if I can call them men – have decided not only to destroy these soldiers but their families as well." Now, Mrs Scott, you told me when I was here that your husband was a soldier who died an honourable death. Would you not say that this was a slander of the dead, and those who are dead are unable to defend themselves?'

Mr Loch looked at her gravely: 'I was struck immediately by what Mr Sellar had told me of your husband, and this is one of the reasons why I am reading you some of these extracts. Please continue, Mr Sellar.'

'Not content with this then, Mrs Scott, Mr Macleod also writes as follows: "It may be true that we are a long-suffering people, and God knows we have been so in the past, and it may be true that our religion has forced us to endure pains which we might not otherwise have been willing to endure. . ." I need read no more. Notice, Mrs Scott, how he blames God for his sufferings. And notice, too, the blasphemous way in which he says, "And God knows we have been so in the past".'

'Thank you Mr Sellar. And now, Mrs Scott, you see the kind of man with whom we have to deal, one who slanders the dead and mocks God. We could read more, much more, of what this godless person has to say. But one other extract will suffice. Mr Sellar?'

'Here is the last extract, Mrs Scott. Though, as Mr Loch rightly says, we could read many more. Please listen: ". . . and we shall have to become robbers and thieves and murderers ourselves in order to fight this oppression." Thieves and murderers. That's what he wants you to become.'

He put the paper back in his case and the two of them looked at her for some time, as if expecting her to say something. Then Mr Loch continued. 'Mrs Scott, after Mr Sellar called on you that night I am sure you must have felt very distressed and very lonely. That is natural. And please believe me when I say again that Mr Sellar is perfectly willing to take the blame for that.'

Patrick Sellar looked down at the floor, then up again.

'These things have to be done but there are ways of doing them,' Mr Loch continued, smiling a little. 'Be sure I gave him a good talking to. Now, Mrs Scott, I am sure that you must have been in great despair. Here you are, an old woman of seventy or more and you do not know what to do. I am

sure Mr Sellar must have explained to you about the new
house and all the conveniences but you couldn't take it all in.
I can understand that. After all, you have lived here all your
days. So when Mr Macleod came to see you and incited you
to go and see the minister, knowing that the minister could
not in all justice help you to do what was wrong–'

'Mr Macleod didn't come to see me. . .'

Mr Loch turned to Patrick Sellar and said in a firmer voice
which at the same time had a queer tone in it which she could
not place:

'But surely, Mr Sellar, you came to tell Mrs Scott about
the decision we had reached that she was to be allowed to stay
here for six months and to receive a pension?'

What was this about a pension and being allowed to stay
six months? Mr Sellar seemed to turn pale, or was that her
imagination? This man was certainly giving it to him.

'Mr Sellar?' Loch stood up to his full height. 'Do you
mean to tell me that you didn't come to inform Mrs Scott of
our decision? Especially after she had been so badly treated
by Macleod? Who turned her against the minister and tried
to influence her decision?'

'I am sorry Mr Loch. . .' How puny Mr Sellar appeared.
'I have been so busy calling at houses. . .'

'This is utterly inexcusable, Mr Sellar. I told you spe-
cifically to go and tell Mrs Scott immediately, then she
wouldn't have been put in such a position by Mr Macleod.
And now that she can help us with Mr Macleod you tell me
that you have been too busy.'

'I told you, Mr Loch, I'm sorry,' said Patrick Sellar,
shuffling uneasily. 'I simply forgot.'

'Forgot! You wouldn't have forgotten if you had been
going to get a pension. Mrs Scott,' he said, opening his arms,
letting them drop and then sitting down again. 'You see what
servants I have. Anyway, now that the matter's cleared up,
we can proceed.'

Outside the window she saw the white horse and the black
cropping side by side, while the sky had turned a coppery
thundery colour.

'Do you mean,' she said, 'that the Duke . . . that I'm
going to get a pension?'

'Yes. And be allowed to stay here for another six months,' said Mr Loch. 'But,' raising his finger and smiling, 'only on one condition – which I will have to tell you about myself since I can't trust Mr Sellar with anything.' Again there was something about the voice. . . 'Now then, Mrs Scott, you have heard me speak of Donald Macleod. In a short time he is to be brought to trial for statements made in these papers which you and I and every Christian must be horrified by, though of course our Mr Macleod thinks himself too good to be a Christian as the rest of us ordinary people are. You can rest assured that I'm telling you no more and no less than the truth when I say that he will be brought to trial within a month. The law is preparing charges now and he will be tried with its full rigour at Inverness. Any friends of his, if implicated in his work, may expect short shrift. For this is now a Government matter, Mrs Scott.' His face becoming very grave he spoke again. 'A Government matter, Mrs Scott. And it will not be in the hands of incompetents like our Patrick Sellar. If found guilty he will be imprisoned and fined heavily. And let me tell you, Mrs Scott, well in advance of any other member of the public, that our law has enough honesty to make sure that he *is* found guilty. Now, Mr Sellar, have you anything to say to Mrs Scott at this juncture?'

'I was merely, Mr Loch, about to advise Mrs Scott that in such a situation it would be wise for her to have nothing more to do with Mr Macleod.'

'Anything else, Mr Sellar?'

'Under your pardon, Mr Loch, I was also going to suggest that she should tell us how Mr Macleod sent her to the minister, knowing full well that the latter has no power or desire to oppose what is legal and right, and how later he took her to his house and used her as a means of stirring up hatred against the minister and the Duke in this village.'

In the distance she could see a cloud full of thunder, black but coppery at the edges, and in the forefront the horses moving restlessly, raising and lowering their maned heads with little snickerings.

'You have missed something out,' said Mr Loch.

'I'm sorry. What have I missed?'

'Mr Sellar has some papers for you to sign, Mrs Scott,
and then you will have nothing to worry about. As we have
said, the minister speaks highly of you. Will you please take
out the papers, Mr Sellar?'

Rapidly, Mr Sellar took them out, went over to the table
and laid them flat, waiting.

'Well, Mrs Scott,' said Mr Loch, looking at her brightly
and keenly. She looked out helplessly into the eye of the
coming storm. The grass was now beginning to stir slightly.
Her hands felt sweaty and unclean.

'Well, Mrs Scott,' said Patrick Sellar, repeating what his
superior had said.

'It is worth saying, Mrs Scott,' said Mr Loch quietly,
'that if you don't sign the papers which, if you like, we will
read to you – and you must remember that they are
Government papers – you will be put out of your house, if
you still persist in your refusal, at the end of two days
exactly. We are beginning to eject tenants on that day.'

'Mrs Scott, we can't wait much longer,' said Mr Sellar.
'Mr Loch has much to do and. . .'

Mrs Scott looked straight into the other room, at the bed,
with the curtains drawn across it.

'No,' she said quietly. And then again she said 'No.'

Mr Loch looked at Sellar, who said frantically:

'But I thought you wanted to stay. You were determined
to stay.'

'I have changed my mind,' she said quite clearly. Is that
what they had come for, to make her betray Donald
Macleod? Their voices were false, all false, like the voice of
the minister.

'No,' she shouted again, then almost screamed, like the
voice that she had been used to hearing once, 'NO.' And
finally, as if exhausted, she said in a lower voice, 'I won't
sign anything.'

'But think of the pension,' said Mr Sellar.

'It is too late for the pension,' she said.

Mr Loch raised his hand.

'Mrs Scott knows what she's saying, Mr Sellar. It's just
that we want to be clear about it. In two days' time she will
have to leave unless she signs this paper. You do understand

that, Mrs Scott?'

'Yes,' she said, quietly without energy.

Mr Loch stood up. 'I see. All right, Mr Sellar, I think we're wasting our time to say more at this juncture.' He walked to the door, Mr Sellar about to speak again, but swallowing the words.

'Two days, Mrs Scott.'

Mr Sellar was now putting the papers back in the wallet unwillingly.

'Perhaps when we come back in two days she'll have changed her mind.'

'Your house will be burnt to the ground, Mrs Scott,' said Mr Sellar angrily.

'It may not come to that, Mr Sellar,' said Mr Loch. 'She has two days to think about it. You can't say that we aren't giving you every chance, Mrs Scott. Come, Mr Sellar.'

Mr Sellar followed Mr Loch half heartedly as if he wanted to say more, and also as if he had failed and would be held to account for it.

'I think it will be a stormy night, Mrs Scott. We'd better be on our way, before the rain comes down. I shouldn't be surprised if there was thunder and lightning as well.'

The two of them went out to the horses – the black and the white – which were stirring restlessly where the grass was being driven by the rising wind. Clouds were now banking black in the west above the hills. There was no sound to be heard apart from the rising wind. The birds had fallen silent. One of the horses reared his head suddenly, shaking it as if he was casting off flies, and she could see the whites of his eyes. His mane was lifting in the racing wind. The other was pawing at the ground with his hooves.

The two men climbed on to the horses with difficulty. The wind was rapidly becoming higher and making a whistling sound. In the centre of the uneasiness she heard a cock crowing. The horses edged sideways as the men mounted, then still moving obstinately sideways seemed to be heading for the shelter of her house. But Mr Sellar produced a whip and lashed his horse once. It dashed forward, racing blindly into the wind, and was followed by Mr Loch's. They rushed into the storm, their hooves sometimes ringing on stone, sometimes muffled by the grass.

When they could no longer be seen she turned away from the window. Lightning flashed about the room, illuminating the dresser and then letting it fall into darkness. She quickly put a cloth on the mirror, in which for a moment she saw her astonished face lit by a sudden sheet of brightness. Thunder rumbled heavily like someone speaking with a deep deep voice and then stumbled onwards from cloud to cloud, a giant walking with one foot on the road and one in the ditch. The furniture was lit and then it went out again. Fire flickered at it and then withdrew like a ravenous tide. Sometimes the dresser was clearly there, then it seemed to disappear. The threatening voice of the thunder rumbled heavy and old as if it had lost its memory, and was followed by these flickering flashes, tongues licking.

She put her hands over her eyes lest she should be blinded. Her father's bearded face looked down at her from the wall. The lightning flickered over her husband's uniform and then left it in darkness. Startled, she heard a cow mooing. Outside, the rope on which she hung her washing bounced up and down.

Then the rain came lashing, the earth bouncing from it. With astonishing rapidity pockets in the ground filled. The road was blind with rain as if it couldn't see where it was going. The whole sky darkened, a level blanket without edges muffling the earth. The thunder and lightning ceased and there was only the drumming of the rain. She got out a bucket, for a steady drip was coming in through the roof. Bang, bang, the raindrops went in the bucket, hitting the sides and rebounding. Eventually it slowed down, like someone becoming quiet after speaking too fast. At last it was a steady drip at longer intervals, not violent, but there all the time like the toothache for which one waited. Plop, plop, it became at last, softer against the rising water in the bucket. And the world stopped heaving and banging. It steadied and returned to what it was, the kind of order it had. The ditches were now full of water and the road full of puddles.

And at last there was silence.

But when she made the tea she felt the teapot shaking in her hand. She looked down at her hand but it wouldn't stop shaking and it was the same with the spoon that clattered against the side of the cup. She drank the tea, even while it was spilling and her hand was refusing to stop its shaking. She held her two hands together, unable to light the lamp for a long time, till they stopped shaking at last. But she had stared into centuries of fear these minutes, into a drenched alien light like the light of fish leaping about in their own element and unknown to man. Her heart was beating in her breast: hammer, hammer, hammer. Finally the hammering ceased and she was out of the sea, stranded on a rock. Safe for the moment.

Another day had passed.

TWENTY

Short and stout and bald-headed, Donald Macleod stood in the doorway, his boots gleaming with rain. She stood up, wondering what he wanted.

'I came over,' he said, 'to see how you were getting on in that storm.' He added, 'Especially after these people had been.'

'Did they go to your house too?' she asked.

'Yes. They gave me two days.'

'Before they came here?'

'Yes.'

'They gave me two days too.'

'Mrs Scott,' he began again after a long silence, looking down at the drops of rain on his boots. 'Can I ask you a favour?'

'What favour is that?'

He paused again, then lifted his head, staring steadily at her:

'I wonder if you would come and stay with us.'

This was the answer to his question, the answer that he had been trying to find, the only answer. And that was it out. He had thought about it very carefully. He knew what he was letting himself in for. At least he thought he did. She would be difficult. As the proverb said, the twist in the old piece of wood is difficult to take out.

'My wife would like to have you, and the children.' He added, 'and I would.'

She looked at him for a long time without speaking. It would be very easy for her, she was thinking, to go with him. She was alone and there would be few to help her in the future. If she went with him someone would be there when she died. She thought again of the way her hands had shaken and wouldn't stop.

A verse from 'Ruth', her favourite book in the Bible, came into her mind. 'Whither thou goest I will go . . . and where thou diest I will die and there will I be buried.' 'No, thank you,' she said, and then: 'Thank you, very much. But I must stay by myself.' Too much had happened to her all these years. She added, 'but if you would help me when I have to move with my furniture.' She decided that she wouldn't say anything about the proposal put to her by her visitors. Some day she might mention it, but not today.

'Of course, Mrs Scott. We'll help you any way we can. We will look after you.' He paused and then asked again, 'Are you sure you won't come?'

'No, Mr Macleod, thank you very much. I'm an old woman now.'

'I see. Anyway, we'll be neighbours.'

'Yes, we'll be neighbours.'

He said: 'And what did your visitors say?'

'Nothing,' she replied. 'They didn't say anything.'

He looked at her half questioningly but decided not to press her further.

'I see.'

She was thinking that it wasn't easy to be tempted by kindness and lies all in the one day.

'You see, Mr Macleod, I have my own ways of doing things. I would try to change but I wouldn't be able to. I wouldn't be good for the children.'

'Why, you were telling them a story when I came in.'

'It was the only story I had, Mr Macleod. I'm not good at making up stories.'

'But what will you do? Will you go to church again?'

'No, I won't go to church. But I'll manage just the same.'

He turned at the door and opened his mouth as if to speak again, but just nodded his head helplessly and went.

When he had gone she went to the bedroom and looked down at the bed. Then staring down at the invisible face she stood there thinking. Perhaps she had beaten it after all, that face, that voice, knowing at the same time that there are far more defeats than victories, and that the victories last only a short time while the defeats last for ever. For as yet she had made only a beginning and there might be no further progress.

You could turn the old proverb the other way and say: There is no high tide without a low tide after it.

But, just the same, things came in on the high tide which you could keep when the tide was going out again.